JAZZ
GUITAR
COMPING

RAISING YOUR CHORD AWARENESS

ANDREW GREEN

Jazz Guitar Comping

Andrew Green

Microphonic Press
500 2nd St. #3
Brooklyn, NY 11215

www.chopsfactory.com

Cover Design: Andrew Green
Interior Design: Derek Olphy

ISBN 0-9700576-4-4

Thanks to:

Jim Hall
John Scofield
John McNeil
J.C. Sanford
Nate Radley
Sarth Calhoun
Matt Pavolka
Diego Voglino
James Clouse

Also by Andrew Green:

Jazz Guitar Technique

BREAKING THE SKILL BARRIER

Microphonic Press • ISBN 0-9700576-1-X

"Andrew Green's book addresses points about Jazz improvisation on the guitar or any other instrument for that matter that are totally on the money and invaluable for all musicians."

John Abercrombie

"I really like Andrew Green's new book, Jazz Guitar Technique. The first half of the book deals with the technique part of it in a very intelligent way. The second half consists of excellent musical examples. The text is simple and concise. I believe this would be a great addition to any jazz guitarist's library."

Mick Goodrick

Jazz Guitar Structures

BOOSTING YOUR SOLO POWER

Microphonic Press • ISBN 0-9700576-0-1

It's funny how you can go for years playing guitar solos based on the same old riffs, feeling like you have hit a wall, and someone shows you one thing that increases your soloing ideas 20-fold.
EVERY PAGE of this book has such a moment.

Online review

CONTENTS

INTRODUCTION

"Comping" is an abbreviation of the word "accompanying". Within a Jazz group, it is the art of improvising a chordal accompaniment for a soloist or singer. When you are the only chordal instrument in the group, you will likely spend 75% of the time comping—which means that it is the most important thing you do.

Much like backgrounds in a big band or orchestra, comping is a musical statement supporting the melody or soloist and filling in when the melody rests. Unlike written backgrounds, however, a comper's chord voicings and rhythms are not predetermined. A modern, interactive comper is continually listening and responding to the soloist and the rhythm section simultaneously, and making rhythmic and harmonic choices that propel the music forward. This is in contrast to an older style of guitar comping that involved playing a chord on every downbeat as a time-keeping function, a la Freddie Green with the Count Basie Orchestra.

Comping rhythms have a tremendous impact on the music, perhaps even more than voicings or harmonic alterations. Because of this, you want to have an overall awareness of the direction of the tune being played and what will enable the soloist to be most effective. For example, if the soloist is playing long, complex lines, the comper might simplify and leave more space so as not to interfere. If the soloist is leaving a lot of space, the comper might interject some melodic or rhythmic statements of his/her own.

The process of learning to comp well is a gradual one, and ideally, one that is never truly finished. Your comping vocabulary will always be expanding and growing, and your ability to interact effectively will increase with experience.

While this book provides many of the tools necessary to comp effectively, it needs to be emphasized that the comper's craft is one developed chiefly by listening and playing. You can gain tremendous insight by listening to great compers and learning their rhythmic and harmonic language. And the single most important thing you can do to develop comping skills is play as much as possible. There is no substitute.

HOW TO USE THIS BOOK

Jazz Guitar Comping can be used as a progressive study of comping or simply as a source of ideas. Although rhythms and voice leading are found throughout this book, they are isolated for study in particular sections.

SECTIONS ON CHORD CONSTRUCTION:

BASIC VOICINGS Learning these chords will be useful when approaching other material in this book.

VOICE LEADING Explains how voices in one chord move to voices in the next chord in a musical way.

MULTI-USE VOICINGS Five voicings discussed in detail showing how each one can be used for many chord types.

VOICING VARIATIONS Variations on familiar voicings and moving one voice within a chord.

PASSING CHORDS How chords outside the basic progression of a tune can be used to connect the chord changes.

HARMONIZED SCALES Furthers the passing chord concept by building multiple voicings from one scale.

INTERVALLIC COMPING Modern, abstract comping using two independent voices.

SECTIONS ON RHYTHM:

RHYTHM An overview of how rhythm shapes comping.

ANTICIPATION/DELAY Increasing the sense of momentum and swing by changing the rhythmic placement of chords.

LONG/SHORT How the length of time each chord is held affects the feel of the music.

CONNECTING Using legato playing to create a different feel.

ARPEGGIATION Adding yet another color to the comping palette.

SPACE/RHYTHM ETUDES Examines how style, tempo and feel influence rhythmic choices.

COMPING ANALYSIS:

STUDIES Transcriptions of recordings featuring four different styles with analysis of the solo and comp.

SUGGESTIONS FOR PRACTICE

1. **Practice with a metronome.** Once you have the fingering worked out for a voicing, practice playing it in time. This will help you to gain fret-hand accuracy and improve your rhythmic acuity and time feel.

2. **Practice one thing at a time.** Working with one new voicing or rhythmic concept exclusively for a period of time will enable you to thoroughly digest its use. Trying to cover too much too fast will slow down the learning process.

3. **Listen as much as possible.** Listening to great compers—guitarists or pianists—will teach you volumes about comping. Although there are technical differences, guitarists can learn a lot from pianists about harmonic concepts, rhythmic placement and filling/leaving space. There are also many more recordings with piano comping than there are featuring guitar.

4. **Play as much as possible.** The best possible way to practice comping is by comping. There are many aspects of comping, interaction/reaction for example, that can only be improved by playing with others.

CHORD SYMBOLS

The following are commonly used chord symbols found throughout this book and elsewhere. Basic voicings for these chords can be found (if needed) on pages 10–11.

Major Chords

C△7   C△6   C Maj7   C Maj6   C⁶₉   C△7+4   C△7+11

C△7♯11   C6

Minor Chords

C-7   C-6   C min7   C min6   C min9   C min11   C min7 sus

Dominant Chords

C13   C7♯9   C7♭5   C7+4   C7♭13   C7   C9   C7+   C7♭5

C11   C7 sus4   C7♭9   C7♭9♭13   C13♭9   C7 alt

(Any combination of b9, #9, #4 and b13)

Minor 7♭5 (Half-Diminished) Chords

C∅   C-7♭5

Diminished Chords

C°   C° Maj7

Chord Symbol Interpretation

The basic chord symbols of a tune are freely interpreted when playing Jazz. For example, if a chord symbol indicates "F" a Jazz player would take that to mean F Major 7 or F Major 9, etc. An F barre chord would almost never be called for. The same goes for 7th chords. C7, for instance, would always be played with at least the 9th or 13th. If C7 is resolving up a fourth, ♭9, ♯9, ♯11, and ♭13 are all freely used. It is the player's choice to determine the appropriate treatment for each chord. In most examples in this book, the basic chord symbol as it would appear on a lead sheet is written above the staff. The chord voicings used in the example will feature all of the above mentioned extensions and alterations.

BASIC VOICINGS

Basic "jazz chord" voicings for the guitar—provided as a reference. If playing in a Jazz context is new to you, or you are uncertain what to play for a particular chord type, learning these chords will help you with the other material in this book.

Major Chords

$G^{\Delta 7}$ $G^{\Delta 6}$ G^6_9 $G^{\Delta 7+4}$ $G^{\Delta 7+5}$ $G^{\Delta 7}$

$C^{\Delta 7}$ $C^{\Delta 6}$ C^6_9 $C^{\Delta 7+4}$ $C^{\Delta 7+5}$ $C^{\Delta 7}$

Minor Chords

A^{-7} A^{-6} A^{-9} A^{-7} A^{-6} $A^{-\Delta 7}$

D^{-9} D^{-7} $D^{-\Delta 7}$ D^{-11} D^{-6} D^{-6}_9

Dominant Chords

C 13   C 7♭13   C 7+4   C 7 sus 4   C 13♭9   C 13♭9

C 13   C 7 alt   C 7 sus 4   C 9   C 7♭9   C 7♯9

Minor 7♭5 (Half-Diminished) Chords

A∅   D∅   G∅   E∅

Diminished Chords

C♯°   B♭° Maj 7   G°   B♭°

VOICE LEADING

Voice leading is the stepwise movement of notes from one chord to the next within a chord progression. This motion creates a sound of inevitable resolution between chords, and is an integral part of western music. It should also be an integral part of comping. Voice leading is what makes comping sound like music, as opposed to a series of random chord voicings.

Based on the way most guitarists learn chords, and the unique layout of the neck, voice leading is not the most obvious thing to do on the guitar. Guitarists traditionally learn that chords are made up of a combination of fingers, frets and strings. Voice leading, on the other hand, requires looking at chords as a specific group of notes played simultaneously, rather than "grips." These notes then connect to notes in the succeeding voicing, etc. For this reason, voice leading necessitates being able to play chords in the same area of the neck, without, for instance, having to jump from the third fret to the tenth and back.

To learn voice leading, start with familiar chord forms and move the notes within them in stepwise motion to notes in corresponding forms. This is more easily accomplished at first with three-note chords than with four or more notes present.

With this in mind, it is often advantageous to leave out the root at the bottom of the voicing. Also, since most group situations involve a bass player taking care of the root function, it's not necessary for you to play it, especially in the lower register. If the absence of the root makes some of the chord voicings unrecognizable or difficult to hear when practicing, add it to the voicing where possible. When playing in a group context however, try leaving it out.

Moving Notes – An Overview

When voice leading through a ii–7 V7 I△7 progression, the most common in Jazz, the notes follow a pattern of motion from chord to chord. (The skill gained from working with this basic progression can be applied to all progressions.) For most chords, the 3rd and 7th provide the necessary information to make the sound recognizable; adding the 5th creates another path of resolution. In the following examples, each of the three voices is first isolated, then shown in context of the voicing. The roots are omitted.

The 7th of A-7 moves down a half step to the 3rd of D7, which becomes the 7th of G△7:

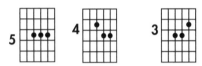

The 3rd of A-7 becomes the 7th of D7, then moves down a half step to the 3rd of G△7:

To create a stronger resolution, tension is increased by altering the Dominant chord. The 5th of A-7 moves down a half step to the ♭9 of D7, then moves down another half step to the 5th of G△7:

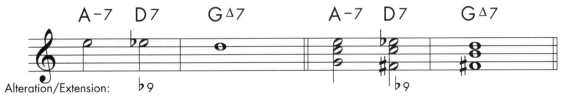

Alteration/Extension: ♭9   ♭9

Voice leading resolving to Minor chords follows similar patterns as those to Major. The ii– chord is often ii–7♭5; the V7 chord typically has alterations such as ♭9.

The 7th of A-7♭5 moves down a half step to the 3rd of D7♭9, then moves down to the 7th of G-7:

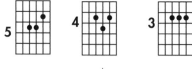

The 3rd of A-7♭5 becomes the 7th of D7♭9, then moves down a whole step to the 3rd of G-7:

The ♭5 of A-7♭5 becomes the ♭9 of D7♭9, then moves down a half step to the 5th of G-7:

Two-Note Voicings

A standard chord progression can be realized with two-note chord voicings made up of the 3rd and 7th of each chord. With a bass player taking care of the root motion, these "shell" voicings supply the necessary voice leading to create a recognizable chord progression. These are often played on the D and G strings:

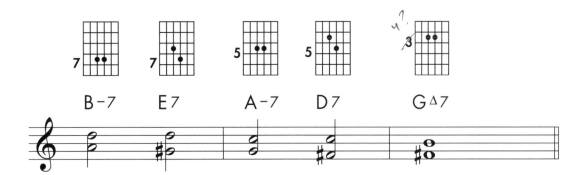

The following uses two-note voicings on a blues progression. Notice that between bars 7 and 8 the voicings jump up a third, then voice lead back down in stepwise motion. If voice leading occurs only in one direction continuously, range problems (too low/high) can occur.

CD
3

Three-Note Voicings

Three-note voicings are very useful in comping. In addition to the 3rd and 7th, the third voice is either the 5th, 9th, 11th or 6th/13th, any of which can be altered when appropriate. These voicings are often played on the D, G and B strings:

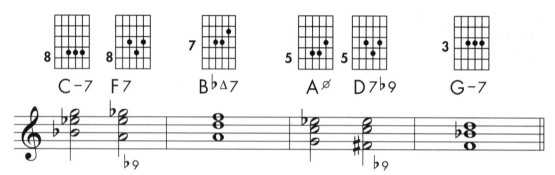

Three-note voicings on a blues progression:

The Upper Voice

The top note in a voicing tends to be prominent, and the movement of that voice creates the "melody" of the comp. The motion of the top voice could be described as one of four things: Half Step; Stepwise; Melodic or Common Tone.

Half Step motion often results from altering the Dominant chord, which creates a strong resolution:

Stepwise motion is also strong and logical:

Melodic motion follows the melody, the other voices move stepwise:

Common Tone, in which the top voice stays the same:

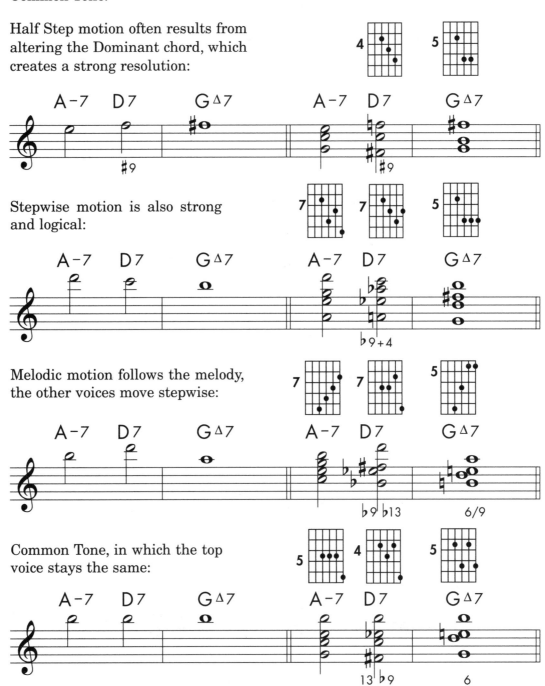

Examples of frequently seen Half Step motion of the
top voice between chords moving around the cycle:

Examples of Stepwise motion of the top voice
between chords moving around the cycle:

Melodic motion of the top voice between chords
moving around the cycle:

Examples of Common Tones in the top voice of chords
moving around the cycle:

Non-Functional Chord Progressions

On non-functional tunes (those with no recognizable key center) and progressions in which chords don't move around the cycle, voice leading is indispensable (since the progressions aren't as familiar). In these situations, voice leading is achieved by utilizing common tones and movement by half step or whole step, as in the following:

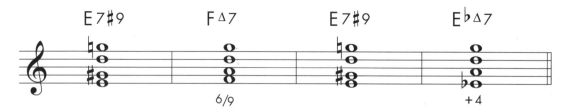

In the above example, the top two voices are common to all of the chords. Note that the chord symbols for FMaj7 and E♭Maj7 are interpreted as F6/9 and E♭Maj7+4, respectively. Since the patterns of resolution are different in non-functional progressions, minor chords can be defined in ways that would not work as well in a ii−7 V7 I△7 progression. In the following example, they are interpreted as minor 6/9:

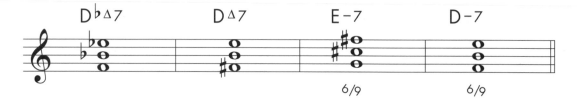

To avoid a voicing that would be out of context within a progression, voice leading can be modified to create greater interest. In the example below, "perfect" voice leading would indicate an A as the lowest voice of the A-7 chord. Since this would create a voicing that doesn't have as much color as the adjacent chords, B is substituted. This creates a voicing with a lot of color and voice leads nicely to B♭ on the E♭-7 chord:

Examples of Non-Functional Voice Leading

MULTI-USE VOICINGS

One of the keys to comping easily and effectively on guitar is being able to use the same chord voicing for many different chord types. This helps to facilitate playing chords in the same area of the neck, and provides more options for voice leading through chord progressions.

The concept of multi-use voicings is in contrast to what guitarists typically learn first—that *one* combination of strings, fingers and frets equals *one* chord type or voicing. For CΔ we play "X" and for A-7 we play "XX", when in fact, many voicings for these chords are interchangeable.

Multi-use voicings have three distinct advantages: 1) it is easier to learn one voicing than twenty; 2) it makes relationships between chord types evident; and 3) it takes advantage of the ease with which guitarists can play parallel chord voicings.

With multi-use voicings, various elements of basic chord sound will not be present in some voicings, which can be advantageous when striving for a more modern sound. This facilitates a broader concept of chord construction—very useful given the limited number of voices available to the guitarist. Strong voice leading and the harmonic context usually resolve any ambiguity resulting from "missing" chord tones.

This section illustrates five chord voicings that can be played for many different chord types, and are easy to grab, move and remember. This concept can then be applied to other voicings as well.

"13th Chord"

The above voicing is one of the most frequently heard sounds in jazz. Used as a three-note or four-note voicing (see below), it is an easy shape to visualize and grab. It is often played on the D–B strings or the A–G strings, with optional notes added to the top or bottom of the basic voicing. It is also played on the G–E strings but with no added notes on top.

The most common use of this voicing is as a Dominant 7 (13) chord. The 9th (A) on top is optional. This voicing works well in ii–7 V7 progressions and for Dominant chords of long duration. When playing with a bass player, the root can be left out.

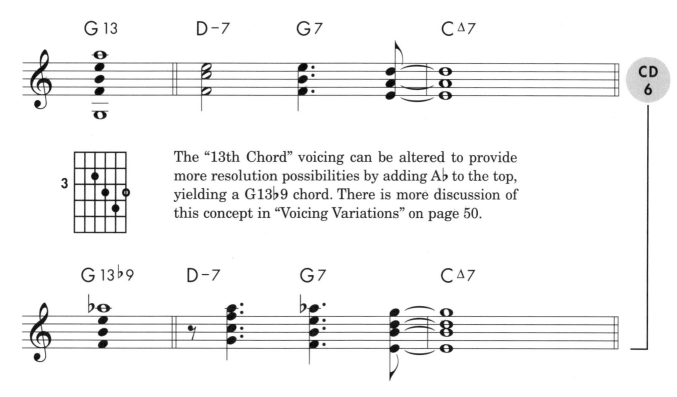

The "13th Chord" voicing can be altered to provide more resolution possibilities by adding A♭ to the top, yielding a G13♭9 chord. There is more discussion of this concept in "Voicing Variations" on page 50.

CD 6

The "13th Chord" voicing can be used as FMa7+4. Here, the root is on the bottom, and adding the A on top (the 3rd) adds basic chord sound.

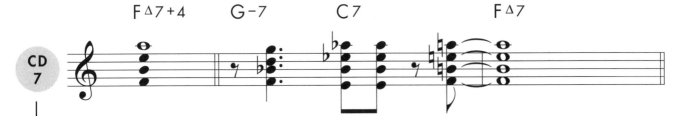

Another function for this voicing is D minor 6/9. This works best on tonic minors, non-functional progressions, modal situations or any time a minor chord of long duration is played. It doesn't work as well in ii−7 V7 progressions, since it sounds like the V7 chord. The root (D) can be added.

This voicing can also be used as B−7♭5 (B∅). Even though the minor 3rd (D) is not present, it still sounds and functions as intended:

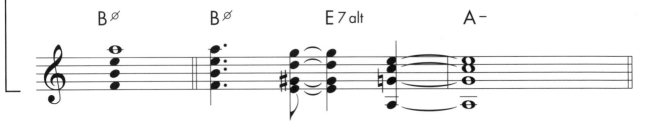

When played over D♭, this voicing functions as D♭7♯9. The root (D♭) can be added to the bottom; the A on top (♭13) is also usable.

CD
8

The "13th Chord" voicing also works as B♭7♭9+4. Notice that playing A on top is *not* an option, since by definition there is no Major 7 on a Dominant chord. A♭ (the 7th) is an option however (see page 25). Most often used when resolving around the cycle:

Over E, this voicing can be used as E7♭9 and G♯ (the 3rd) is an option on top of the chord. This voicing allows for color and tension on a Dominant chord when the root is in the melody. Most often used when resolving around the cycle:

Since it doesn't define the 3rd, another use for the 13th chord voicing over E is E-7 phrygian. This is most commonly heard in modal situations:

Examples Using the "13th Chord" Voicing

By taking advantage of its different possibilities, the "13th Chord" voicing can be used to play through many chords in a progression. To demonstrate, the example below uses this voicing in parallel to play every chord.

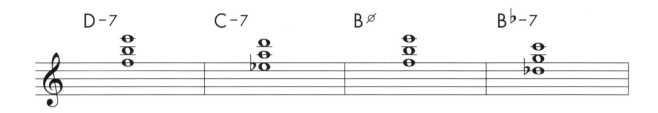

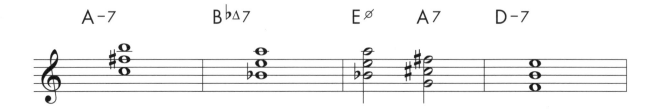

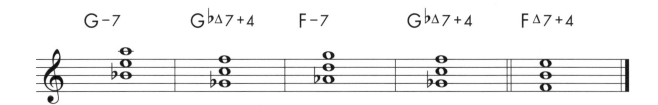

Minor Blues

Major Triad

The Major triad—a barre chord minus the barre. It is shown here on the D, G and B strings, and can also be played on the top three strings. This voicing would rarely (practically never) be used as a C Ma chord as is, since it lacks any of the color notes typically heard in Jazz. It also works when the triad is played in other inversions.

To create a usable C Ma7 chord, add B to the top of the voicing:

This is also one of the most basic voicings for A-7; just add an A on the bottom or the top. Playing a B on top yields A-9.

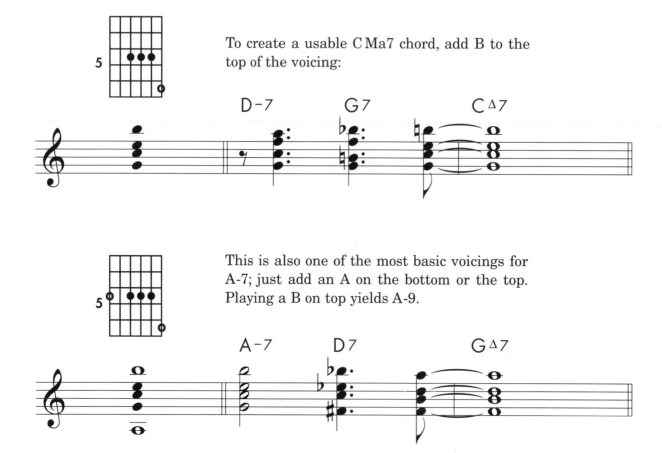

When played over F, this voicing is a distinctive sounding F Ma7 chord. The whole step between F and G and the absence of the 3rd give this voicing its characteristic sound.

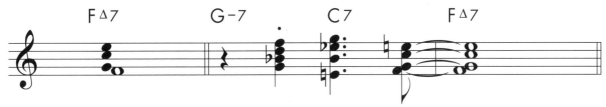

As with many Major chord voicings, the above also works for the relative minor, D minor. To be most effective, the F should be present.

Play a C triad over D to get D7sus4. This works well any time a Dominant 7sus4 chord is called for. Also notated as C/D.

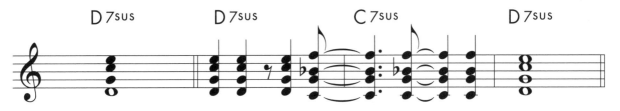

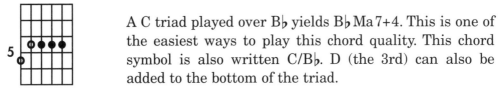

A C triad played over B♭ yields B♭Ma7+4. This is one of the easiest ways to play this chord quality. This chord symbol is also written C/B♭. D (the 3rd) can also be added to the bottom of the triad.

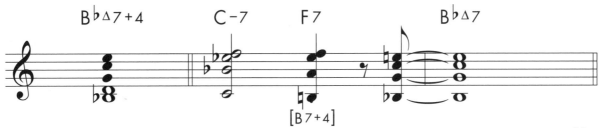

Another use for a C triad is over A♭, which creates A♭Ma7+5. This is an option for Ma7 chords that can tolerate a "darker" color. This chord symbol is also written C/A♭.

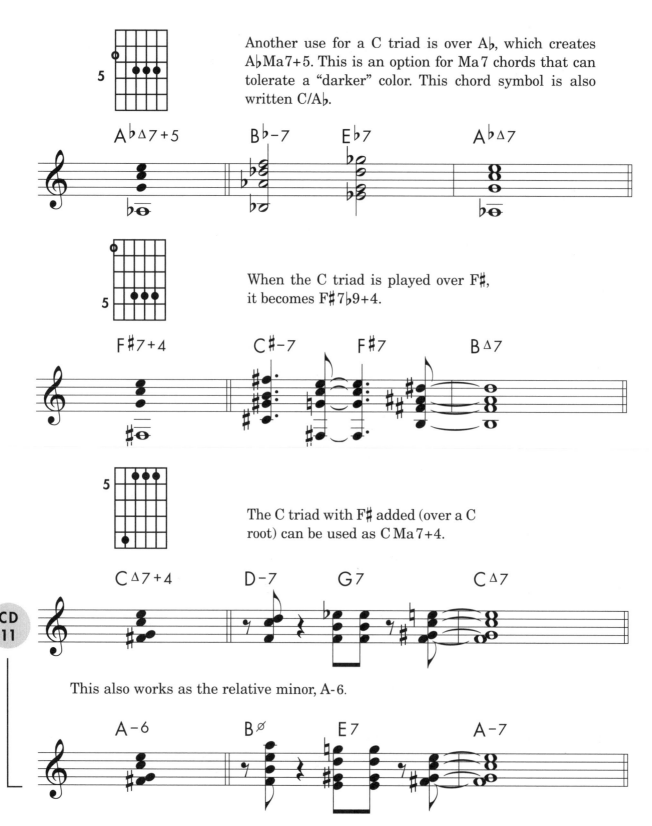

When the C triad is played over F♯, it becomes F♯7♭9+4.

The C triad with F♯ added (over a C root) can be used as C Ma7+4.

This also works as the relative minor, A-6.

This voicing over C♯ yields four chords in one. The first is C♯°(Ma 7). This works in many situations when a Diminished chord is needed.

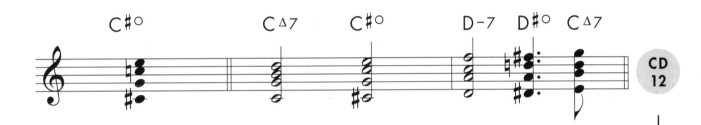

It also produces A7♯9...

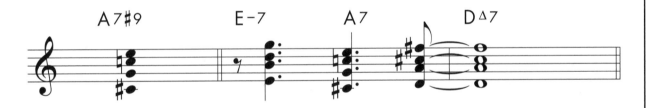

...as well as E♭13♭9 (when played over D♭)...

...and C 7♭9 (when played over D♭).

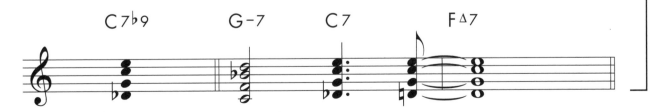

Examples Using a Major Triad

"Major 7th" Voicing

Another voicing with many applications is made up of a half step and a major third. This is a very "thick" sounding chord voicing that is used frequently by piano players. Given the stretch involved, it is most easily played on the D, G and B strings.

This is a very useful voicing for C Ma 7.

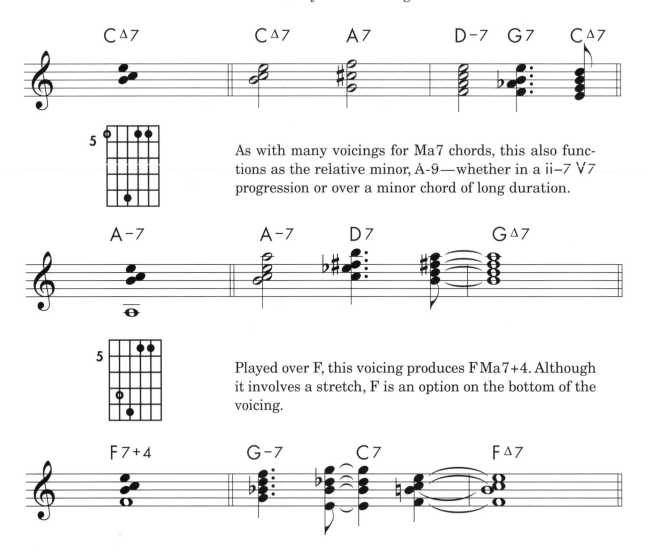

As with many voicings for Ma 7 chords, this also functions as the relative minor, A-9—whether in a ii-7 V7 progression or over a minor chord of long duration.

Played over F, this voicing produces F Ma 7+4. Although it involves a stretch, F is an option on the bottom of the voicing.

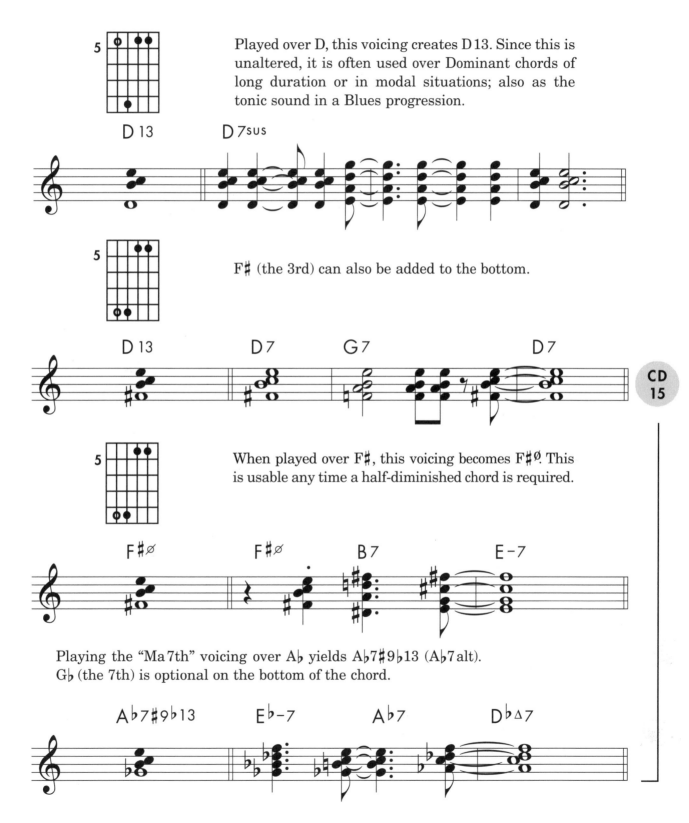

Played over D, this voicing creates D13. Since this is unaltered, it is often used over Dominant chords of long duration or in modal situations; also as the tonic sound in a Blues progression.

F♯ (the 3rd) can also be added to the bottom.

When played over F♯, this voicing becomes F♯⌀. This is usable any time a half-diminished chord is required.

Playing the "Ma 7th" voicing over A♭ yields A♭7♯9♭13 (A♭7 alt). G♭ (the 7th) is optional on the bottom of the chord.

Examples Using the "Major 7th" Voicing

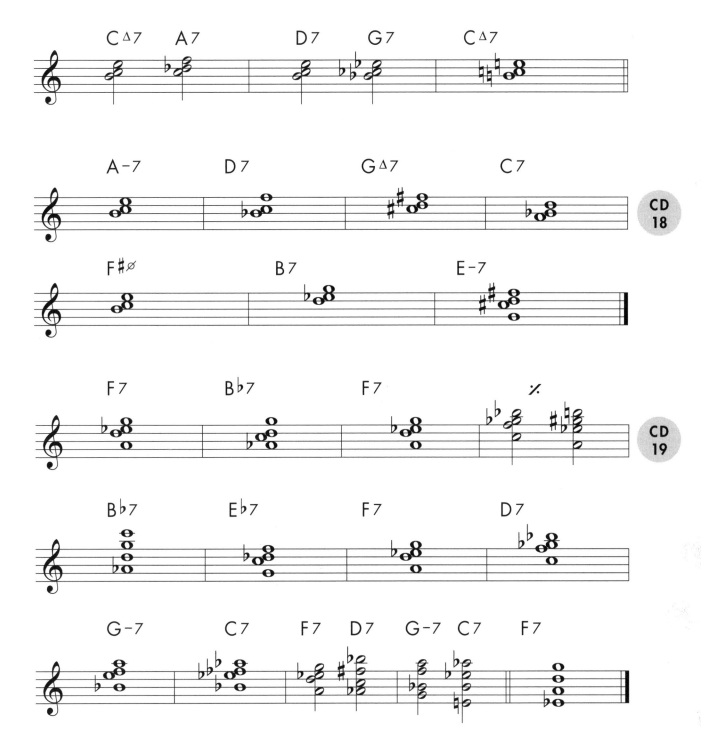

Fourths

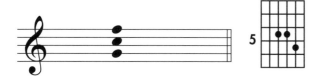

Voicings made up of consecutive fourths are among the most frequently heard sounds in modern Jazz. Since their basic sound is ambiguous (not obviously major or minor), voicings in fourths are useful for playing many different chord types. They are also easy to grab and move up and down the neck. The voicing is shown here on the D, G and B strings and can be played on any three consecutive strings.

The most common use for this voicing is D-7 with the 11th added. This can be used in most situations in which a D-7 is called for. Adding A on top creates the "So What" voicing, after the tune of the same name.

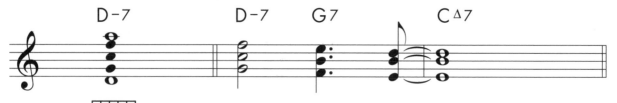

Although it doesn't define the third unless B♭ is added to the top, a voicing in fourths works as G-11 (also G7sus without B♭).

Playing this voicing over E♭ yields E♭ 6/9. This chord can be used as an alternative to Ma7 chords in many situations. B♭ can be added to the top of the voicing.

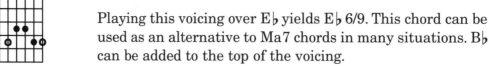

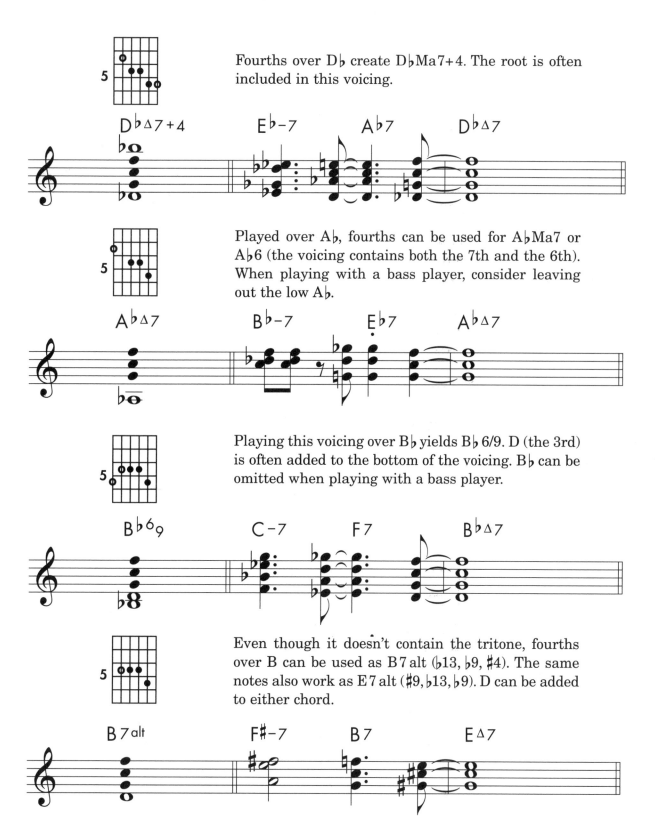

Fourths over D♭ create D♭Ma7+4. The root is often included in this voicing.

Played over A♭, fourths can be used for A♭Ma7 or A♭6 (the voicing contains both the 7th and the 6th). When playing with a bass player, consider leaving out the low A♭.

Playing this voicing over B♭ yields B♭6/9. D (the 3rd) is often added to the bottom of the voicing. B♭ can be omitted when playing with a bass player.

Even though it doesn't contain the tritone, fourths over B can be used as B7 alt (♭13, ♭9, ♯4). The same notes also work as E7 alt (♯9, ♭13, ♭9). D can be added to either chord.

Examples Using Fourths

"Diminished Scale" Voicing

A voicing made up of minor 3rd, minor 3rd, perfect 4th (A triad over B♭ root) creates an altered Dominant chord. This voicing, derived from the Diminished scale, is used primarily over Dominant chords that resolve around the cycle (also over Diminished chords). Because of the stretch involved, it is easiest to play on the top four strings; the middle four are also possible.

As with any Diminished scale structure, this voicing can be moved up or down by minor thirds (parallel) and still function as the same chord—only the alterations change:

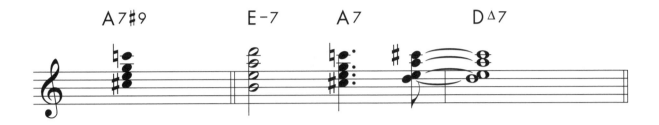

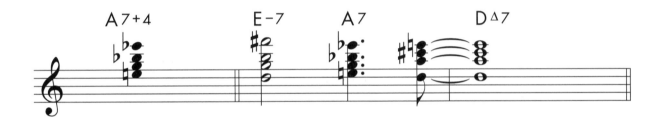

Alternatively, each of the previous voicings can be used for Dominant chords built on *roots* that are a minor third apart, *i.e.* A7, C7, E♭7 and F♯7:

The "Diminished Scale" voicing can also be used for *Diminished chords* built on roots a minor third apart. Note that the roots are a half step above those used for the Dominant chords above.

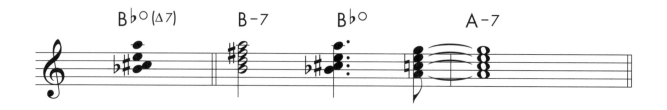

The "Diminished Scale" voicing has several variations that are closely related—it's just a matter of changing one note (see "Voicing Variations" on page 50). Three of these variations can be used in the same way as the "Diminished Scale" voicing.

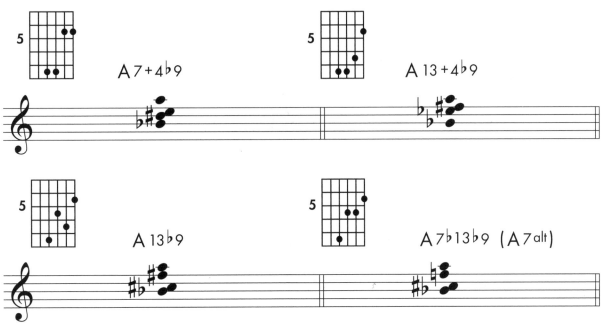

Since this voicing is from the Altered scale, the same applications don't apply.

Examples Using the "Diminished Scale" Voicing

VOICING VARIATIONS

Guitarists typically learn that one combination of fingers, strings and frets equals one chord voicing; if a note is changed, it's an entirely different chord. This can be misleading, and needlessly complicates the learning process. When it comes to comping effectively, it's easier to think of one voicing as having three or four closely related variations than as three or four completely separate chords. Here's an example using the "13th Chord" voicing from page 25.

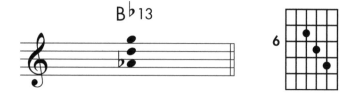

One of four easily playable notes can be added to the top of this voicing: D♭, the ♯9; C, the ♮9; B, the ♭9; and B♭, the root.

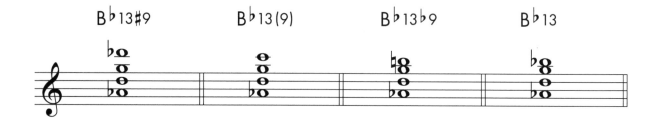

Over a B♭7 resolving around the cycle, the ♯9, ♭9 or both might be used. Over a Dominant chord of long duration or when used as the tonic chord in a blues progression, ♮9 or the root would be likely choices.

These notes can be held for the duration of the chord...

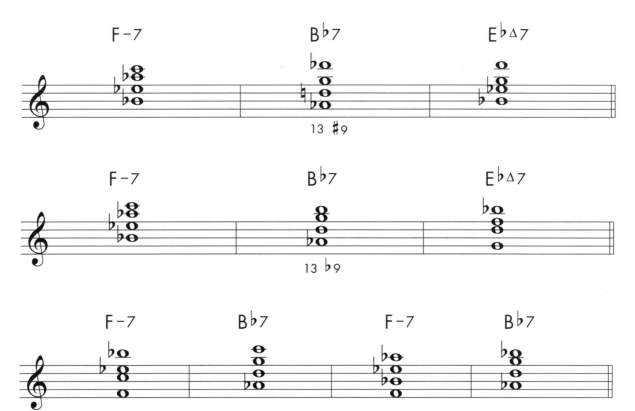

...or, any combination of these notes can be used as an independently moving line against the rest of the voicing. This provides movement in an otherwise static situation—especially useful at slow to medium tempos. When your fingers need to shift to accomodate the moving voice, play the entire voicing again.

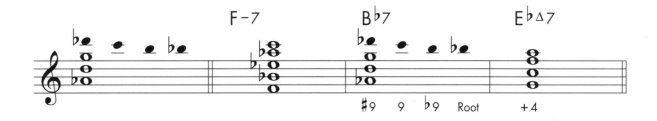

Dominant Chords

Since they feature notes not commonly found on other chord types, Dominant chords have the most possibilities when creating variations.

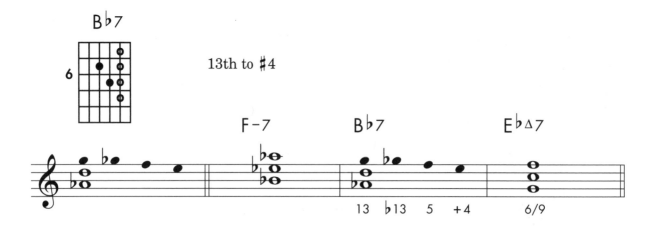

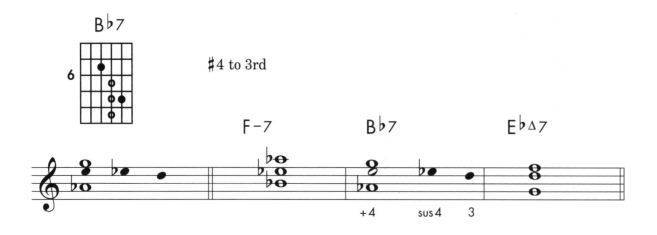

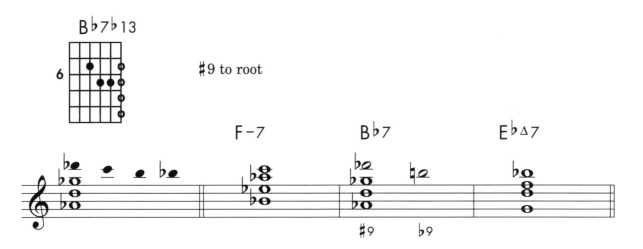

♯9 to root

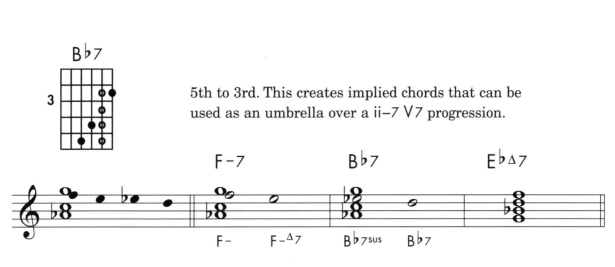

5th to 3rd. This creates implied chords that can be used as an umbrella over a ii–7 V7 progression.

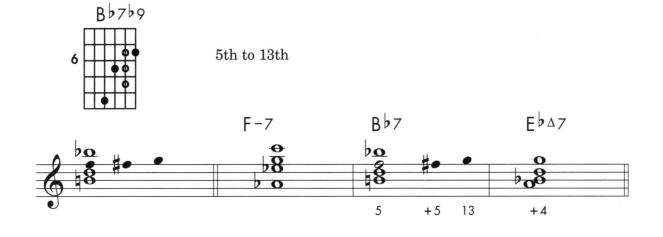

5th to 13th

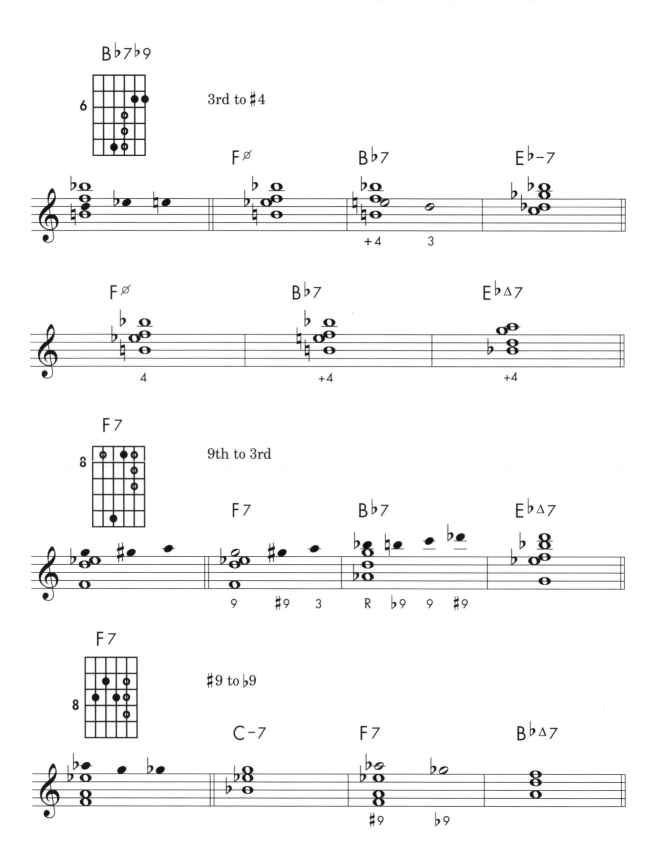

Major Chords

Over major chords, motion is possible between the 3rd and ♯4, 5th to 6th, 6th to 7th, and root to 9th. Many of these voicings also work over relative Minor chords.

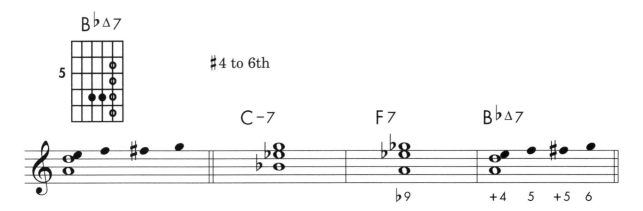

In some cases, the ♯5 will imply a superimposed Dominant (see "Passing Chords" p. 62).

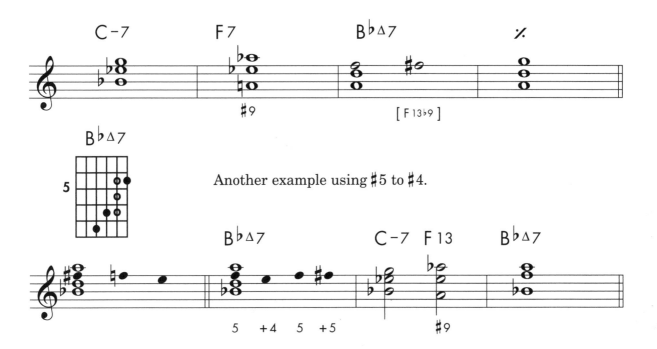

Another example using ♯5 to ♯4.

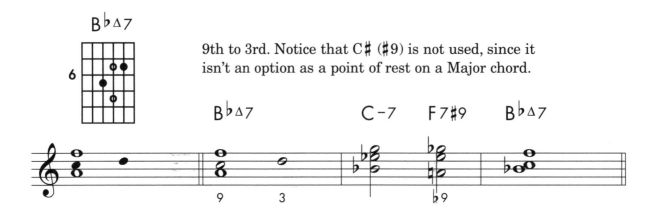

9th to 3rd. Notice that C♯ (♯9) is not used, since it isn't an option as a point of rest on a Major chord.

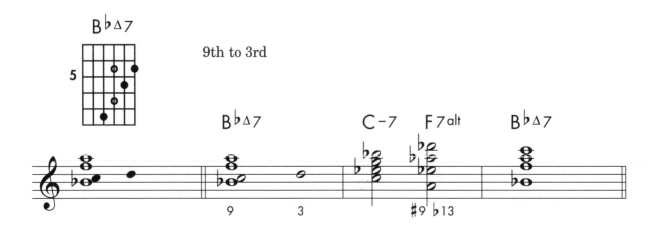

9th to 3rd

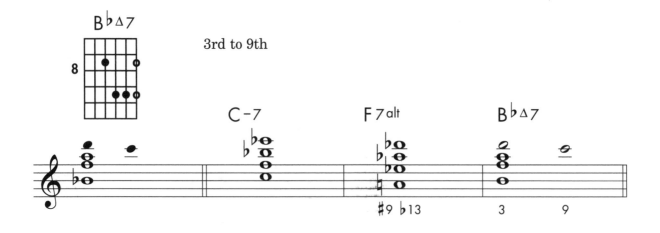

3rd to 9th

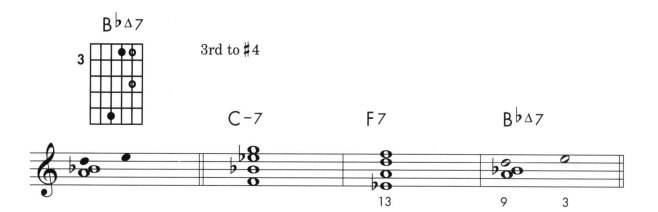

Minor Chords

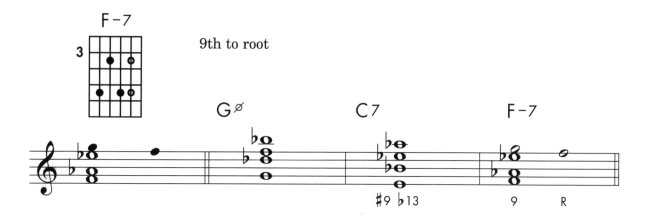

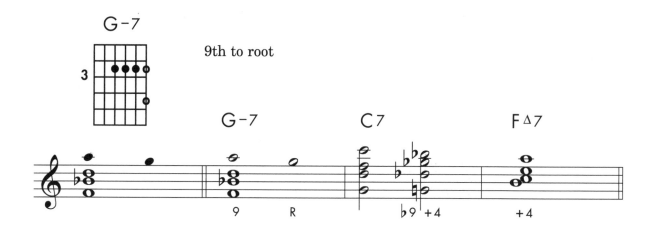

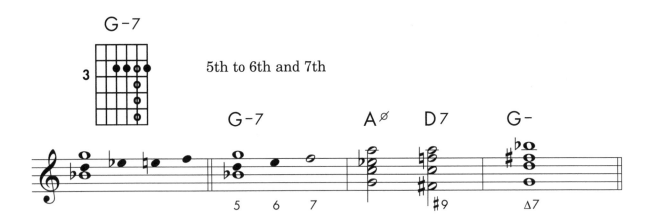

5th to 6th and 7th

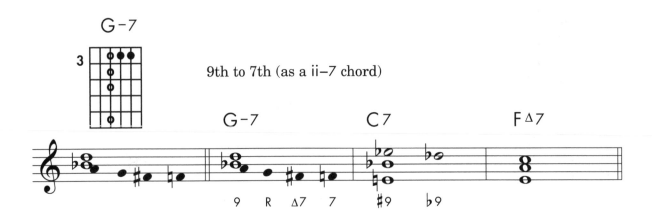

9th to 7th (as a ii–7 chord)

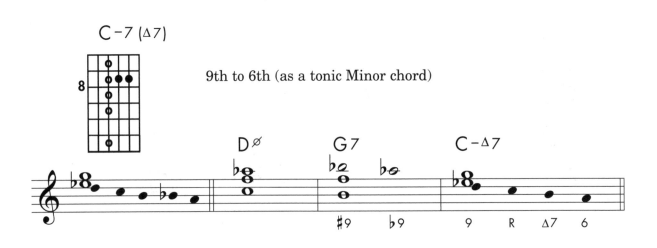

9th to 6th (as a tonic Minor chord)

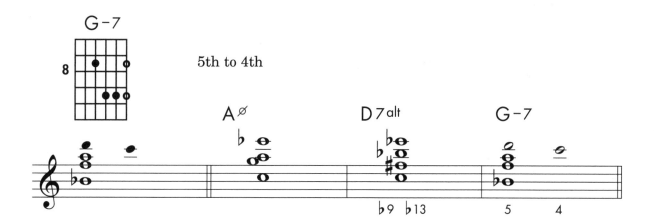

5th to 4th

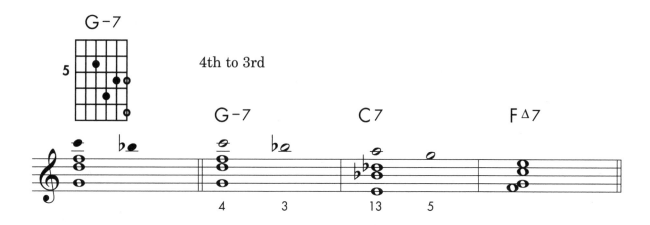

4th to 3rd

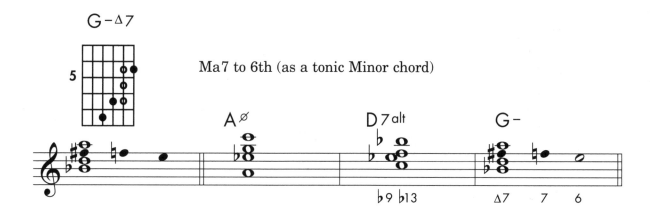

Ma7 to 6th (as a tonic Minor chord)

Ballad with Voicing Variations

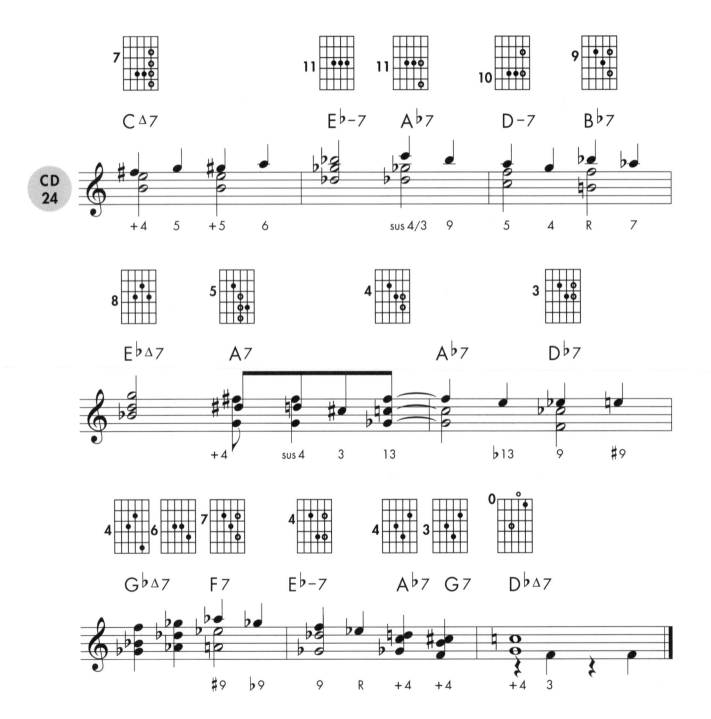

Medium Tempo Tune with Voicing Variations

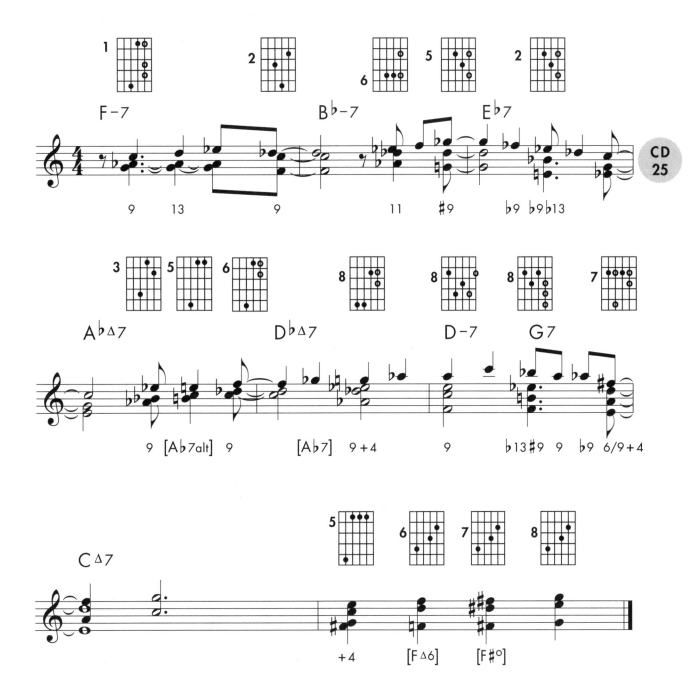

PASSING CHORDS

In order to create motion and stronger resolution patterns in a comp, chords from outside the basic progression of a tune are used to form connections between the written chords. These "passing chords" are, by definition, not held or extended, as in using alternate chord changes—they are used "in passing." When listening to an experienced comper, you will hear passing chords being used frequently.

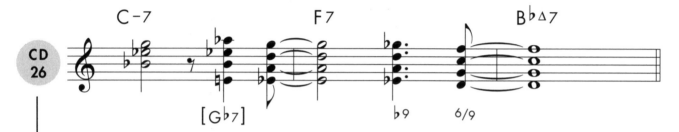

In the above example, G♭7 (the tritone substitution for C7) is a passing chord between C-7 and F7. The momentary tension created by the passing chord against the underlying chord, and the movement of each note by a half step, results in a strong resolution to F7.

This use of substitute Dominants is one of the most common passing chord devices. This can be done more than once in a progression:

Parallel chromatic chords are often used in passing, in this case, Minor7s:

In the previous example, the C♯-7 passing chord creates movement in what would otherwise be a static point in the progression. This also works ascending:

Another use of a chromatic Minor 7 passing chord—in this case, approaching from above:

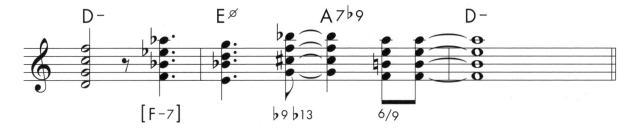

Dominants also work well ascending chromatically:

Dominants moving chromatically, with the top note staying constant:

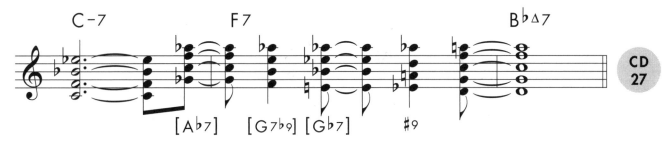

CD 27

Although they're not held long enough to be considered reharmonizations, Minor 7 chords can be paired with substitute Dominants to create passing ii-7 V7s:

Major 7 chords can also be used as chromatic passing chords from above or below:

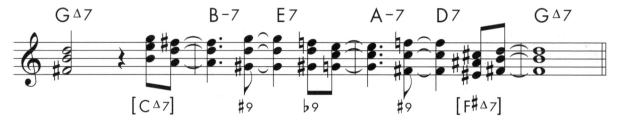

Since playing the same voicing for the entire duration of a multi-measure chord or modal section would become monotonous, superimposing a passing Dominant or parallel chromatic Minor 7s can be used to create motion where it wouldn't exist otherwise:

Non-diatonic parallel chords can be used to create a moving pattern in a modal context:

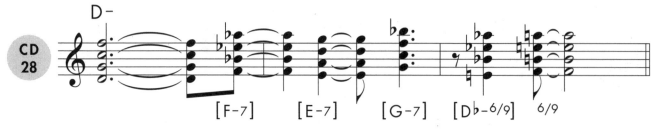

Blues Progression with Passing Chords

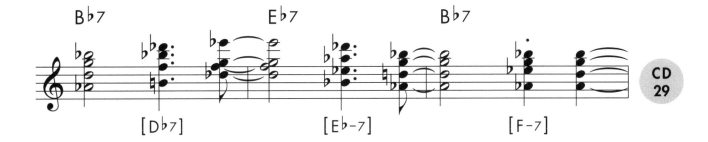

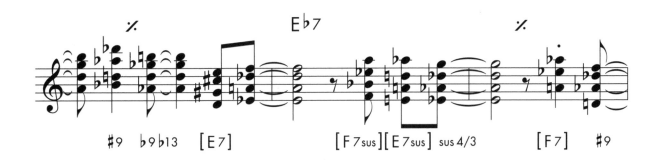

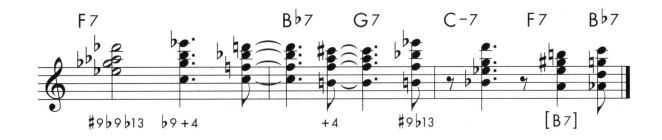

HARMONIZED SCALES

One way to achieve motion within a comp is to use harmonized scales. These are created by building a voicing on each step of a scale, using only notes found within that scale. To maintain a cohesive sound, each chord is built from consistent (not parallel) intervals.

Among its uses is solving the problem of how to create interest when playing the same chord for an extended duration. For instance, rather than trying to find five different C-7 voicings, this technique creates seven different voicings derived from the C-7 (Dorian) scale.

The following is a Dorian scale harmonized with voicings in fourths:

Some voicings have more basic chord sound; some act as passing chords. Notice that when the scale dictates an augmented fourth, the voicing contains that interval.

In the following example, the Dorian scale is used over C- in a modal context:

In this example, the harmonized scale is used to create motion over the C-7 within a ii–7 V7 I△7:

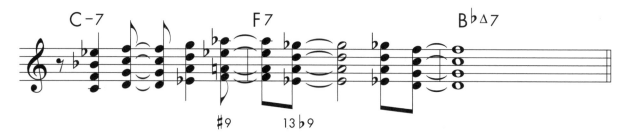

Once a scale is harmonized, the voicings for the other modes of that scale are already in place. For example, to create a Phrygian sound, play C Dorian chords over a D root, starting with the voicing built on D:

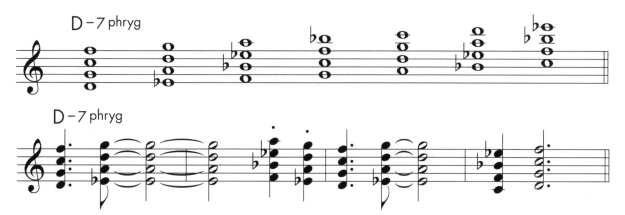

Over Major 7 chords, there are two primary options. The Major scale (Ionian) is mostly used when the soloist is playing diatonically over the chord. The voicings with the 4th contained within them (such as the voicing built on the root) are used as passing chords rather than points of emphasis.

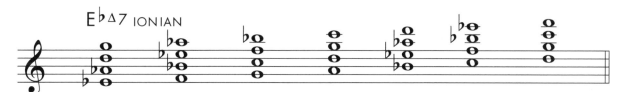

When harmonizing with the Lydian mode (Major 7♯4), all voicings are available as points of emphasis.

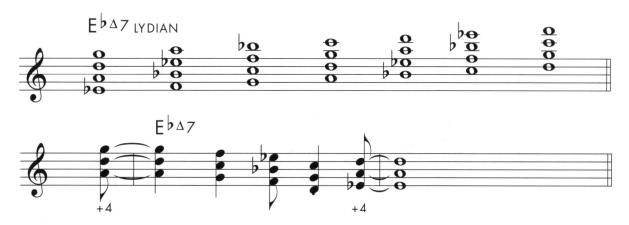

Since Myxolydian has a ♮4, the voicings containing B♭ will imply a sus 4 sound.

Myxolydian ♯4, the fourth mode of the Minor △7 scale (Melodic Minor), is a good alternative over Dominant chords. In this example, it is voiced in fourths and a third:

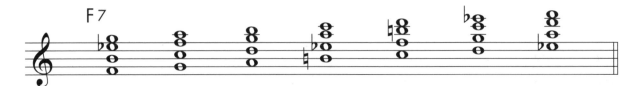

Here's an example of Myxolydian ♯4 over one chord:

For Minor 7♭5 (Half Diminished) chords, use the sixth mode of the Minor △7 scale; the voicing built on the fifth degree has the most chord sound:

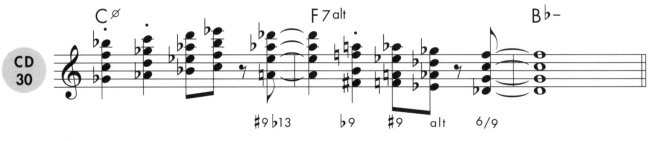

CD 30

The following uses the harmonized Altered scale (7th mode of the Minor∆7 scale) over D 7:

A harmonized Diminished scale alternating between two voicings. In this example, the voicings share a note to create more chord sound:

As shown on page 44, the above scale would also be used over E♭7, F♯7 and A7.

The following examples compare harmonized Altered and Diminished scales:

Altered Scale (♭13)

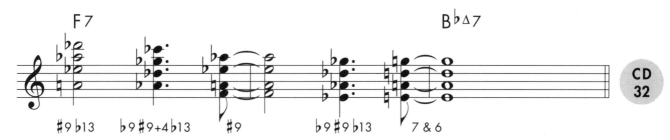

Diminished Scale (♮13)

Although chords built in fourths have been used up to this point, there are numerous ways to harmonize the same scale. The following is a C Dorian scale harmonized with different interval combinations. The voicings below could be used for any of these chords symbols:

C–7   E♭△7+4   F7sus   D–7 phryg   A∅

Whole step and fourth

Fourth and whole step

Fifth and third

Two-note voicings can also be effective:

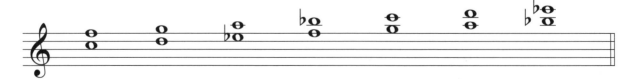

The following is an example of a ballad comp using harmonized scales and occasional passing chords:

INTERVALLIC COMPING

Intervallic comping consists of moving voices only, with no pre-determined chord forms. This approach creates an improvised background which can incorporate counterpoint-like ideas. Since it gives the music an introspective quality, rather than a swinging rhythmic feel, it is typically used more for the melody or first chorus of a solo. It also works well on ballads.

Intervallic comping usually involves two voices. The smaller number of voices opens up the harmony, allowing the soloist more freedom of expression and the group an overall more modern sound.

Limiting the number of voices necessitates defining chords in different ways. In contrast to "shell" voicings (page 15), note choices are not limited to outlining basic chord sound. Consider an altered Dominant chord defined by the 3rd in the lower voice and the ♯9 in the upper voice resolving to a Major 7 chord defined by the root and Major 7th:

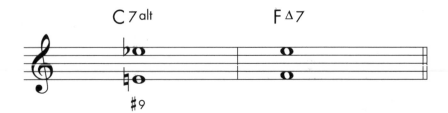

Even though no 7th is present in the Dominant chord and no 3rd is present in the Major chord, effective voice leading and resolution still happen. Depending on the interval involved, two notes can sound thicker than if additional chord tones were present—particularly for the Major 7 chord.

With intervallic comping, the interval between the two voices and their relationship to the root determine the nature of the sound. A major 9th is the widest usable interval—larger intervals tend to be less effective. This means that there is a finite number of usable intervals, which can be grouped according to how "dense" they sound. The scale choices are the same as those illustrated in "Harmonized Scales" on pages 66–71.

Major and minor 2nds and 7ths, along with tritones and ♭9s create the most tension and therefore sound the "biggest":

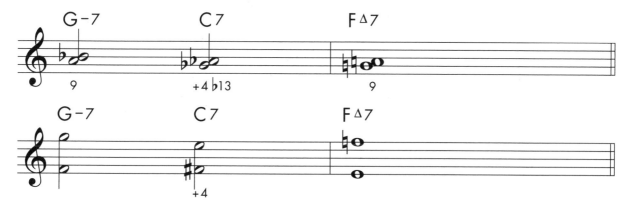

4ths, 5ths and ♮9ths are somewhat ambiguous, depending on the relationship to the bass note. On a Dominant chord, 5ths and 4ths built on the ♭9 or ♭13 are very effective:

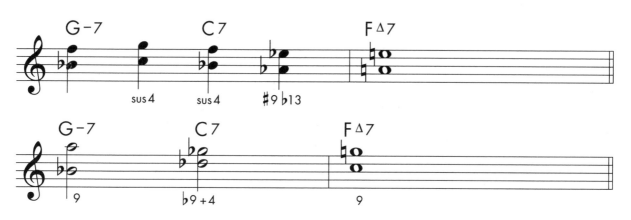

3rds and 6ths sound very familiar and "inside":

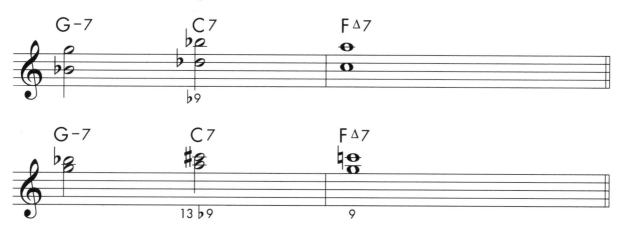

Intervallic Examples

The following is an example of a background with voices moving independently; common tones are used to create prhases across the bar line.

CD 34

RHYTHM

The function of a comping instrument is to listen to the soloist and provide the best possible framework for his/her conception, and rhythm is the key element in providing this support.

The comping instrument in a Jazz group traditionally interacts the most with the soloist and the drummer. Since the bass player typically plays a line of predominantly quarter notes outlining the harmony of a tune, much of the interaction that happens between the comper and the bass is in the form of improvising the same reharmoniaztions.

The drummer keeps time on the ride cymbal and plays accents on the snare and/or bass drum. These accents constitute comping, and the comper should hook up with the drummer and vice versa. If both players are listening and responding to the soloist, and to each other, they will often play in the same places. The more familiarity the players have with the Jazz idiom, and the more they play as a group, the more likely it becomes that the rhythmic hook-up will happen.

When it comes to rhythm, the best way to learn its usage as part of the language of Jazz is to listen and then imitate great players of any instrument, not just guitar. In particular, good drummers have a tremendous amount to teach any musician about rhythm, time keeping and comping.

From a rhythmic standpoint, comping behind a soloist can be seen as following a continuum of interaction. At one end, comping involves playing rhythms that are grounded in the Bebop tradition (see pp. 80–81), which is a less obviously interactive way of comping. The principal comping hook-up in this style is with the drummer; much of the interaction that takes place with the soloist in this context is harmonic, *i.e.* adding a sharp fourth to the chord if the soloist is heard to do the same. This style of comping is mostly supportive, creating a background for the soloist and filling in when the soloist rests.

At the interactive end of the continuum, there are a greater number of choices as to how to respond to the soloist. This approach can be more like an active dialogue between soloist and rhythm section. For example, if the soloist is playing a staccato, pointillistic solo, the comper could play short chords in imitation of the soloist or sustained non-rhythmic chords to create contrast.

Regardless of the level of interaction called for by the style, there is always a question of how much space to fill up. If the soloist is playing long, complex lines and leaving little space, the comping instrument typically plays less. If the soloist is playing notes of long duration or leaving rests, the comp can be more active. How much you play will depend on the mood of the tune and your own (and the group's) aesthetic.

When comping is broken down from a rhythmic perspective, there are four basic variables:

1. Where chords are played in relation to the underlying progression

2. How long the chords are held

3. Whether or not to connect each chord to the following chord

4. How much space to fill up in a particular passage

The following pages illustrate some basic principles about how to deal with these rhythmic variables, and provide some exercises to practice them.

Anticipation/Delay

Playing a voicing on the downbeat of every chord change would quickly become predictable and therefore boring. One way to create interest and swing is to play some of the chords on the eighth note or quarter note before the actual chord change. Play and compare the following examples:

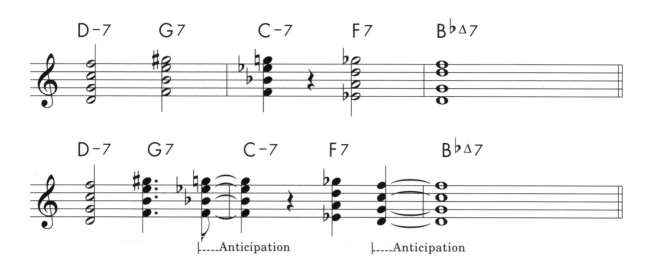

The first example has little sense of motion, whereas the anticipations give the sense of being propelled forward, which creates excitement and swing.

Another rhythmic option is delaying the attack of a chord by an eighth note or quarter note. When combined with anticipation, delaying provides further interest:

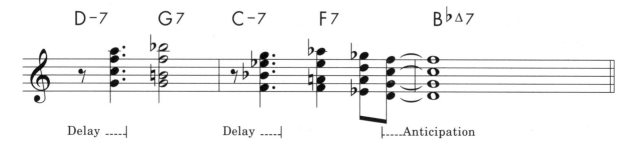

In the following example, note the effect of delaying combined with downbeat and anticipated attacks when comping under an eighth note line:

The principle effect of both anticipation and delay is that chords occur on, and accent, the up beats. This is one of the things that gives Jazz its characteristic sound. It should be noted that *too much* delay can sound indecisive.

When listening to players who have a thorough knowledge of the Jazz language, you will hear anticipation and delay used constantly. The best way to learn how to do this effectively is to listen to experienced compers; over time, playing these rhythms will become second nature.

The following pages feature examples/exercises for practicing anticipation and delay

Basic comping rhythms from the Bebop tradition featuring
anticipation and delay.

Basic comping rhythms—anticipating the first chord

Comping Etude   mm: ♩ = 144

Comping Etude   mm: ♩ = 100

CD
37

Long Notes and Short Notes

After deciding where to play a chord, the next consideration is how long to hold it. The timing of the release of a chord contributes as much to the comping rhythm as playing the chord in the first place.

Compare the feel of these two examples:

Since both examples use the same voicings and placement, the length of the notes is what creates the difference in feel.

One consideration to keep in mind is that some soloists like to hear a chord first and then play over it. In this case, sustained chords may be called for. Other soloists would rather have the comping respond to them, and consequently, shorter attacks might be used.

Since using just one or the other would soon become predictable, a combination of long and short notes makes for more interesting comping:

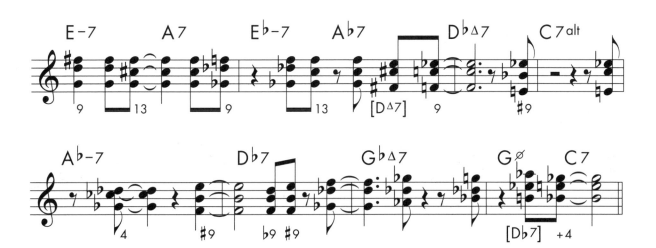

Different tempos will also influence the length of notes. The following example is at ballad tempo, using predominately sustained chords, with short chords providing contrast:

The following exercises contain long and short chords:

Minor Blues using a combination of long and short chords:

CD
38

Connecting Chords

Typically there is a brief rhythmic gap when moving from voicing to voicing on guitar—as soon as the fret hand fingers are lifted, the chord stops sounding. Connecting chords with no perceivable gap in between—known as "legato" playing is one way to add to the number of rhythmic options.

To connect chords, the following technical issues need to be addressed:

1. Every finger of the fretting hand has to leave the first chord and arrive at the second simultaneously.

2. The voicings have to be in the same area of the neck in order to connect them. You can't easily connect two voicings that are eight frets apart, since the physical distance would be too great to work consistently.

3. Generally, three-note voicings are the easiest to connect. Four-note voicings are also possible. Five-note voicings are considerably more difficult.

While the actual rapidity of movement of the fret hand fingers is the same at all tempos, it is easiest to practice connecting chords at medium tempos. At slow tempos there is simply more time between movements, and the possibility of the chord ceasing to ring is greater; at faster tempos there is more frequent movement.

Following are some exercises to practice connecting chords; they start simply and proceed to more complex examples.

Arpeggiation is a comping device that is more often used to create impressionistic mood than to achieve swing or rhythmic drive, and works well on ballads and rubato passages.

This technique involves grabbing a chord voicing as usual but playing the notes in the voicing one at a time, often letting each note ring. Since there are multiple attacks involved in playing each chord, arpeggiation is not always appropriate for passages in which the melody or soloist is very active rhythmically.

Executing arpeggiation with a pick can present a technical challenge. To get around this, the thumb and three fingers can be used in approximation of classical technique.

In the following example, the notes in each voicing are played lowest to highest, maintaining voice leading. The triplets add to the mood and work well with three-note voicings.

Notes played high to low, again maintaining voice leading:

Repetitive eighth-note triplets create more motion than quarter note triplets (let all notes ring):

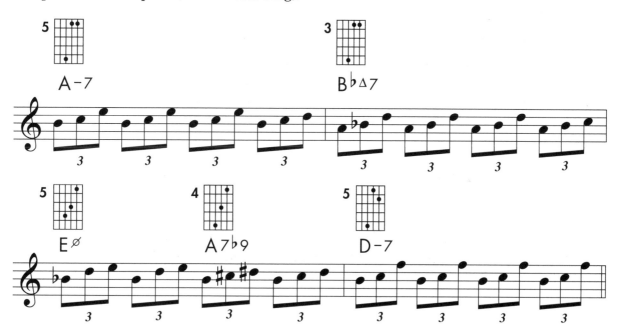

A moving eighth note line with voice leading happening at changing rhythmic intervals (let all notes ring):

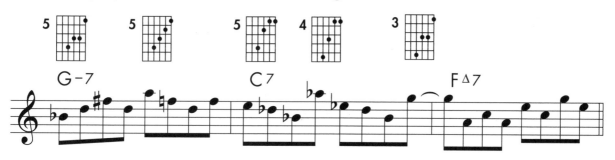

A combination of arpeggiated and simultaneously played chords.

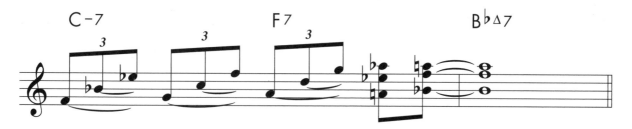

Space

Deciding how many attacks to play in a given framework of measures is largely a matter of aesthetic choice. Factors that will influence your decision include tempo, your technique, the style or feel of music and the preference of the soloist(s). There is no "right" or "wrong" choice apart from what your ears are telling you.

One area in which the comper has a lot of options is in between the soloist's phrases or places where the melody rests. The following is a comparison of two approaches to playing a bebop style turnaround at a medium tempo, in which the soloist leaves space until the top of the following chorus. The first example is a basic statement of the chords, leaving space. The second example illustrates a counter-melody played with chords, which is rhythmically active:

Relatively sparse:

Relatively active:

The musical circumstances and your taste will determine which approach is most appropriate. Tempo will also have a major influence on how much you play in a given measure or phrase. At slow to medium tempos, you have the option of playing more attacks per measure. At faster tempos, playing too much leads to a busy feeling and is difficult to execute.

For learning purposes, most examples in this book feature a voicing for every chord in a progression. In actual practice, some chords could be omitted, particularly the Minor 7 in a ii–7 V7 I△7 progression. The following demonstrates effective comping without playing every chord in a progression:

The following etude is played at a slow swing tempo. Notice that there are many chord changes, and that much of the resolution is non-functional. Over progressions of this type and at these tempos, the comp can be relatively dense, and the use of sustained chords is more frequent than in a bebop context.

The following etude is played at a medium swing tempo. Stylistically, this tune is in the bebop tradition, and the progression uses both functional and non-functional resolutions.

CD
41

The following etude is played at a fast, modern swing tempo. On tunes featuring multi-measure changes and fast tempos, a lot of space can be used. There is often activity at the transition from chord to chord, creating a feeling of tension and resolution.

The following etude is a modern ballad with a combination of functional and non-functional resolutions. There is frequent use of triplets, sometimes oocurring in unusual places, and sustained chords and legato playing are stylistically appropriate. This would be played behind a soloist who was sustaining notes and/or leaving a lot of space.

97

The following etude is a bossa nova, which features rhythms that are more or less consistent (with a few variations). In order to maintain the feel of the rhythm, no space is left.

The following etude is played at a medium tempo with an even eighths feel, and featuring a combination of modal and nonfunctional harmony.

STUDIES AND ANALYSIS

The following studies feature a soloist and comping—
analyzing voicings, rhythm, response, etc.

Blues in F

Analysis starts on page 102.

This is a bright medium tempo blues in F. The style of performance could be called "modern mainstream." There are many elements of the bebop tradition present along with more modern elements. The solo makes great use of Pentatonic scales and reharmonization with Lydian and Altered scales while maintaining a strong connection to the blues.

Chorus One: Measures 1 – 4

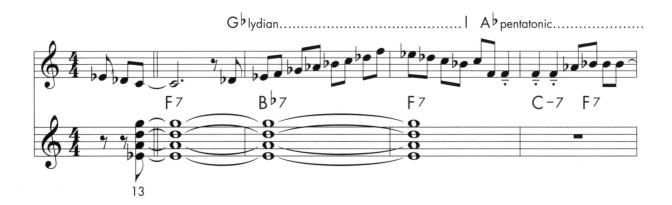

At the beginning of the solo, both soloist and comper anticipate the downbeat. The soloist is rhythmically active in bars 2–3, and reharmonizes with G♭ Lydian (implying an altered dominant resolving to F7); begins A♭ Pentatonic phrase anticipating B♭7 at the end of bar 4.

Since the soloist is playing an extended eighth note line for much of the first four bars, the comp is not actice rhythmically. The guitar voicing is an unaltered dominant that establishes the tonic and treats the phrase as a modal passsage, without playing B♭7. This is an example of the comper letting the soloist establish the direction of the solo. There is no interaction to speak of.

Measures 5–8

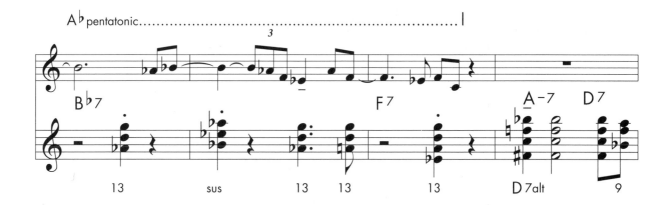

The soloist uses an A♭ Pentatonic umbrella from bar 4 into bar 7, much like using the Blues scale but without the ♭5. The phrase uses a combination of sustained and short notes.

The comp uses unaltered voicings in bars 5–7 and D 7 alt in bar 8 (omitting the A-7). Rhythmically, the guitar plays short attacks against the sustained trumpet notes, and uses a common bebop motif consisting of an attack on beat three of bar 5—short (delay of the B♭7); on beat one of bar 6—short; on beat three of bar 6—long; and on the "and" of four of bar 6—short (anticipating the F7). This type of motif eastablishes a pattern for the listener, then breaks the pattern, which creates suprise and interest.

This rhythmic motif is an example of what could be called the "Three Rule." The pattern starts with three on-the-beat attacks, two beats apart. If an attack was played on the downbeat of bar 7 instead of the "and" of four of bar 6, it would be predictable, rather than suprising.

As a rule of thumb, this holds true for many motifs—three times feels okay, the fourth time seems predictable. The guitar starts the pattern again on beat three of bar 7, but changes it by playing on beat two of bar 8, creating further suprise.

In terms of interaction, the comp, using short chords, fills in space exactly opposite to the solo: trumpet anticipates the downbeat of bar 5, guitar plays in the space on beat three; trumpet on 4 "and", guitar on beat one of bar 6. Trumpet and guitar line up rhythmically on beat three and the "and" of four of bar 6, anticipating the downbeat of bar 7. The trumpet leaves space at the end of the phrase (bar 8) and the guitar fills it up, anticipating the G-7 in bar 9.

Measures 9–12

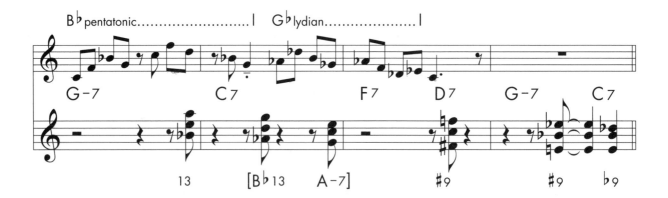

The soloist plays a rhythmically active motif of ascending fourths/descending thirds using B♭ pentatonic over G-7 and G♭ lydian over C7 extending into a delayed resolution in bar 11, and rests in bar 12. Note that the change in scale doesn't happen exactly in line with the chord changes, but is staggered across the barlines—a sign of an experienced player.

The guitar voicings are unaltered until bars 11 and 12, with each attack anticipating the next chord change. B♭7 is used as a passing chord connecting C7 and A-7 in bar 10. The D7 takes a ♯9 voicing, the G-7 isn't played, and the C7 moves from ♯9 to ♭9.

Since the trumpet is very active, the comp is not busy. All chord attacks are short, leaving lots of space for the trumpet line. The guitar plays a rhythmic pattern anticipating beats one and three of bar 10, and beat one of bar 11. Instead of anticipating beat three of bar 11, the attack is delayed by a quarter note to anticipate beat four instead. The "Three Rule" again.

Second Chorus: Measures 1–4

The soloist plays diatonic motifs in F major for bars 1-3 (substituting G-7 C7 for Bb7), then reharmonizes, outlining the tritone substitute for F7 (B7) starting on the third of the chord, in bar 4. Rhythmically, the motif accents beat three in bar one and an eighth note sooner in bar 2.

The guitar plays F13 followed by a parallel voicing up a minor third (see page 44) creating F7b9 (b9, 5 and root) and matching the last trumpet note. The F13 voicing in bar 4 is unaltered but contains a half step. Even though the pitches don't precisely outline the same alterations as the trumpet, the tension created by the half step is in line with the tension created by the reharmonization.

Rhythmically, the comp answers the soloist in bars 1 and 2. The motif accents beat three in bar 1 and the "and" of beat two in bar 2. The comp paralells this by playing on beat four of bar one and the "and" of three in bar 2. The guitar leaves space in bar 3, and plays a motif in bar 4 that will recur later in the chorus: beat one—short, beat two—long.

Measures 5–8

The soloist starts a motif of descending fifths moving down in whole steps that continues into bar 10. The strength and logic of the motif makes it work even though notes in some cases are not explicitly outlining the underlying harmony. It begins with two-measure ideas using a descending fifth followed by a scalar idea. The motif is drawn from the B♭ myxolydian scale over B♭7 and the D altered scale as an umbrella over F7 | A-7 D7 (bars 7 and 8). The motif is varied rhythmically in bar 8 by using triplets instead of eighths.

The comp rests in bar 5 and plays a B♭7+4 voicing using the beat one—short, beat two—long motif. In bar 7, the guitar uses a whole step/4th voicing to play D7 altered, leaving out the A-7. The E♭ on top of the voicing matches and answers the trumpet, and the B♭ below it is the inverse of the descending fifth.

Rhythmically, the guitar answers the fifths of the trumpet motif and, having recognized a pattern, rests in the second scalar phrase to avoid interference.

Measures 9–12

The trumpet motif continues from bar 5. It outlines altered C7 as an umbrella over the ii–7 V7 in bars 9 and 10. The B natural, technically a "wrong" note against C7, resolves as the leading tone to the 5th of F7. The strength of the motif also creates a sense of rightness for the listener that outweighs any other consideration. This motif goes against the "Three Rule" melodically but applies it rhythmically. It begins with the descending fifth appearing every two bars for the first two units, starts to do the same in the third unit, then plays the figure a measure early, creating suprise. Bar 12 uses a G♭ Lydian scale resolving to ♯4 of F7 anticipating the top of the next chorus.

The guitar continues following the trumpet with whole step/4th voicings, outlining C7 altered in bar 9. The voicing used for F in bar 10 is ambiguous (doesn't contain a 3rd, 7th or anything else specifically defing an F7. The C on top of the voicing matches the trumpet, and could be said to have something of a sus chord sound. The voicing in bar 12 is C7♯9 using the beat one–beat two motif, again not playing the ii–7 chord.

Standard Tune

Analysis starts on page 110.

This is a 32-bar ABAC form taken at a relaxed tempo, and very much in the bebop tradition.

Intro

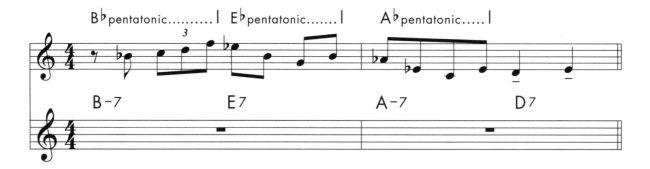

The solo break reharmonizes the turnaround, outlining B♭Ma7 E♭Ma7 and A♭Ma7—a variation on a classic Bebop device.

Measures 1–4

The trumpet starts motivically—half step ascending, jumping up to a whole step descending. *Over the B♭-7 E♭7 in bars 3 and 4, the chromatic is an approach note rather than a scale tone. The motif varies rhythmically between the two units, the second being shorter.

The guitar uses an interval-based voicing, adding a third note on the "and" of beat four. The B♭-7 voicing uses a natural 13. This works because the resolution of the ii–7 V7 is non-functional. The voicing is made up of a fourth and a second, and is used to harmonize a B♭ Dorian scale in bars 3 and 4.

The guitar sustains underneath the first unit of the trumpet motif in bars 1 and 2, and fills in leading to the second, anticipating the B♭-7. The guitar sustains in bar 3 when the trumpet is active and fills in the space in bar 4 when the trumpet rests.

Measures 5–8

The soloist starts a new motif and seamlessly transitions into a bebop line based on the fifth mode of the A harmonic minor scale, used as an umbrella over the Bø E7 in bars seven and eight.

The comp picks up the opening GΔ7 voicing and shifts to standard, less "modern" voicings in bar 6 to respond to the developing direction of the tune. The E7 is treated as E7♯9 moving the top voice down to ♭9.

Rhythmically the guitar continues the pattern of anticipating and sustaining in bars 5 and 7, and punctuating in bars 6 and 8. The comp is relatively sparse behind an active solo that includes extended eighth note lines.

Measures 9–12

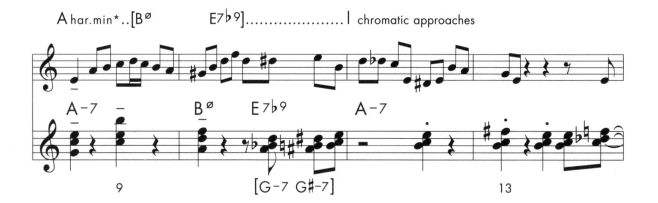

The trumpet solo continues the extended eighth note bop line that began in bar 7. The line outlines A-, and anticipates Bø and E7♭9 (starting from the 3rd, following the practice of not arpeggiating Dominant chords from the root). *Chromatic approach notes are introduced in the second half of bar 10, first approaching the root of E7 followed by the 3rd and 5th of of A-7. The trumpet then rests in bar 12.

The guitar uses standard voicings for A- in bar 9 and Bø in bar 10 then the "Maj 7th" voicing with chromatic passing chords approaching A- in bar 10. Even though it is only a three-note voicing, it fills up a lot of the sonic spectrum of the group and sounds full. In bar 12, the top voice of the "Ma 7th" voicing is moved up to the 13th then back to the 5th. The voicing is moved up a half step to be used as E♭13, anticipating bar 13.

Rhythmically, the guitar is active but uses short chords that leave space behind an active solo. One of the positive aspects of this choice of note length is that for six of the eleven attacks in these four measures, the top note of the guitar voicing is a half step away from the trumpet melody. If the guitar chords and the melody were sustained, it would clash. As it is, any dissonance is barely noticed.

Measures 13–16

The soloist plays a classic Bebop scale line (Myxolydian with the chromatic between the root and the seventh) in bars 13–14, and uses the root and 2nd as approach notes to the 5th of A-7 on the downbeat of bar 15. The D Altered scale is used to voice lead the ♭13 of D7 to the 9th of GΔ7.

The comp uses the "Maj 7th" voicing as E♭13 under the eighth note line in bars 13–14. Even though there are only three voices present, a voicing containing a half step creates a thicker sounding texture which can sustain for the entire two measures. A passing D♭ triad is used as B♭-7 moving down a half step to a C triad as A-7, anticipating bar 15. The D13+4♭9 voicing is from the Diminished scale; D7♭13♭9 from the Altered scale, exactly paralleling the trumpet by voice leading to the 9th of GΔ7.

The soloist and the comp playing the same melody in bar 16 is a function of the players speaking the same language. The familiarity of the players with the idiom and the experience of having played together a great deal contributes to these moments when everything lines up exactly.

Measures 17–20

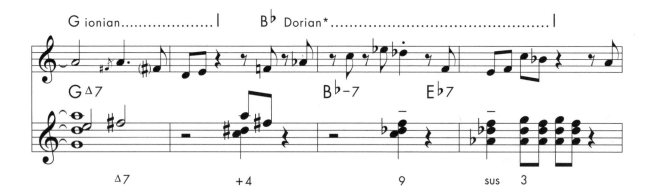

The trumpet resumes motivic playing that echoes the contour of the first four bars of the tune (over the same chord changes). The figure consists of sustained tones followed by staccato attacks, anticipating the Bb-7 in bar 18. Bar 18 features the same approach note concept and melody as that used in bar 3, with rhythmic variation. The soloist's recall of the earlier parts of the solo creates a sense of form (theme and variations). The ability to do this when improvising is the mark of a very experienced player.

The guitar voicing matches the trumpet melody and moves the 6th up to the 7th. The "Ma7th" voicing is used for GΔ7+4 in bar 18, with a variation moving from the 9th to the 7th, and is moved down a half step to funtion as Bb-9 in bar 19. A Db triad is used as an Eb7sus4 voicing in bar 20, with the top note moving from the 9th to the 3rd.

Rhythmically, the guitar sustains in bar 17 matching the solo and answers the trumpet in bar 18. The moving note against the chord in bar 20 matches, then answers, the end of the trumpet phrase.

Measures 21–24

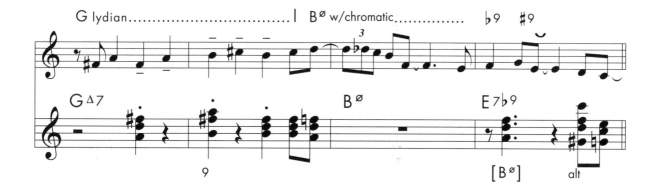

The soloist plays a melody with legato quarter notes ascending using the raised 4th against the GΔ7 in bar 22, then anticipating the Bø, and descending gracefully through the iiø V7 using E7♭9♯9, resolving down to the 3rd of A-7.

The guitar voices the GΔ7 using a D triad, moving up to a B-7 and back before anticipating Bø. In bar 24 the E7♭9 is treated as a delayed iiø V7, then anticipates A-. The E7alt voicing is one of the only four-note chords in the entire chorus.

The comp uses a standard bop rhythmic device in bars 21 and 22 (see page 103) which lines up perfectly with the quarter note melody of the trumpet solo; both comp and solo anticiapate the Bø in bar 23.

Measures 25–28

The soloist pauses in bar 25 after an active descending legato melody. Continuing the legato motif in bar 26, the root of E7 is approached chromatically (above and below); jumps up to the ♭13, which resolves to the 9th of A- in bar 26; arrives at the root in bar 27 (delayed resolution); and continues down through the the C-7 F7 in bar 28.

The comp uses standard voicings in bars 25 and 26, with E7 being treated with ♭9 ♯9. Multiple chromatic passing chords are used to connect A-7 and C-7. The melody of the comp jumps up to the 9th of the C-7 chord for emphasis, matching the trumpet note, and beginning a descending phrase that will run the rest of the chorus.

Most chords in this phrase are anticipated by an eighth note. The guitar punctuates the space in the solo in bar 25, loosely matches the trumpet rhythm in bar 26, and fills in rests in bars 27 and 28.

Measures 29–32

After a protracted lyrical statement, the soloist returns to an eighth note-oriented bop ending. The line uses misdirection in bar 29 by ascending to the +4 of E7 (as opposed to the more usual 7 to 3 resolution). As in bar 16, the soloist makes use of ♭13 on D7 alt resolving to the 9th of GΔ7. Bars 31 and 32 use arpeggiation, approach notes, and an E- structure (5, 7, 9 of A-) moving to an E♭- arpeggio (from the D Altered scale) over the A-7 D7 in bar 32. The root and 7th of the E♭- act as approach notes to the 5th of GΔ7 on the downbeat of the next chorus.

The guitar uses a ♯9 over the E7 in bar 29, a C triad for A-7 and a standard D7(9) voicing in bar 30. The "Ma7th" voicing, in parallel, is used to cover the start of the turnaround in bar 31 up to the A-9, then switches to a voicing made up of 3rds and 2nds for D7 alt and GΔ7+4. The rhythms are the same pattern used in bars 21 and 22, here used twice consecutively.

The guitar corresponds rhythmically to the trumpet on eight out of nine attacks—a result of knowledge of the language, time spent playing as a group and listening.

Modern Changes

Analysis starts on page 120.

This tune is more modern in conception: much of the harmony is non-functional; extensive use of Pentatonic scales, fourths and intervallic playing. The overall rhythmic feel is more open, not as much in the Bebop tradition, and the slow tempo means greater possibilities for rhythmic subdivision.

Intro

The soloist ends the previous chorus by using D♭ Pentatonic over B Ma 7 in a long ascending/descending line—creating a strong blues reference. The guitar plays a sustained B△7 voicing.

Measures 1–4

The solo begins with a motif based on an intervallic mode made up of 4ths and 2nds, used as an umbrella over E♭7 and D 7 alt. Fourths, along with a descending G- triad in bar 2 are used to cover both the G-7 and A♭△7. The quarter notes over the A♭△7 are the 7th and 3rd. Continuing into bar 3, fourths are used as the ♯4 and 7th of the B△7, and the 5th and 9th of D7. The motif rests in bar 4. The use of long then very short attacks creates a melody that is both lyrical and humorous.

The comp uses basic E♭13 and D7♯9 voicings in bar 1, followed by the "Ma7th" voicing for G-9 and a voicing made up of a second and a fourth for A♭△7. The "Ma7th" voicing is again used in parallel for B△7 and D13 in bar 3. Bar 4 also uses voicings made up of a second and a fourth to harmonize a D Dorian scale, using arpeggiation. The rhythm of the comp follows the soloist's lead in playing on-the-beat attacks in bars 1–3, anticipating that the arpeggiation in bar 4 would contrast with more quarter notes in the trumpet melody. Since the trumpet rested in bar 4, the arpeggiated figure instead became a counter melody.

Measures 5–8

The trumpet solo continues with fourths, this time consecutive ascending to F, then repeated down a whole step to E♭. A blues treatment of the Dominant chords in bar 7 accents D♭ then C in bar 8. The top note of each figure creates a descending scale line. This is an excellent example of using simplicity and space over a complex chord progression with functional and non-functional resolutions.

The comp resumes use of the "Ma7th" voicing in parallel for E♭13, D13 in bar 5. Bar 6 reprises the same voicings as in bar 2. In bar 7, a basic 13th voicing followed by F7♭13 voice leads down to the 9th of B♭7 in bar 8. The eighth note group at the end of bar 8 uses a B♭7+4 voicing with a moving note on top going from the 5th to the 13th. Having started this phrase using rhythms similar to the first four bars, the comp responds to the rhythmic change instigated by the soloist by using shorter attacks. The top note of the guitar voicings matches the emphasized melody notes of the trumpet solo exactly in bars 7 and 8. The moving note group at the end of bar 8 fills in the space at the end of the trumpet phrase.

Measures 9–12

On the bridge, the trumpet continues the blues-influenced idea, using basically B♭ Dorian as an umbrella, much like the Blues scale, over both the E♭7 and B♭7. At the end of bar 11, a Diminished scale figure is used to anticipate a resolution back to E♭7. The rhythms in this phrase are very active, in contrast to the space and feeling of the first eight bars. This is a good example of the rhythmic variation possible at a slow-medium tempo.

The comp starts with a moving top note over a basic 13th voicing harmonizing an E♭ Myxolydian scale. The next voicing in the scale is an E♭7sus4 with the 3rd also present (notated above as E♭7sus/3). At the end of bar 10, the bottom voice of the previous chord is raised a half step to the ♯4. Over B♭7 in bar 11 a B♭13 +4 voicing punctuates the end of the solo phrase. A passing E13 chord is used at the end of bar 12 to move to E♭13, anticipating the next bar.

Behind a very active trumpet phrase, the comp uses sustained chords and lots of space, mostly emphasizing the transitions between chords and listening for the ends of the trumpet phrases. The eighth notes at the end of bar 12 are picked up from the rhythmic figure played by the bass (not transcribed).

Measures 13–16

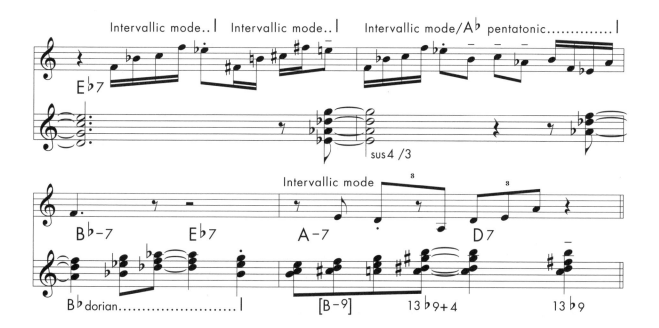

In the second half of the bridge, the solo again uses an intervallic mode which repeats up a half step (implying a substitute Dominant function). The motif is repeated in the first key before dovetailing into an A♭ Pentatonic line. The figure in bar 16 is also based on an intervallic mode, and serves as a sort of "capper" to the phrase. The trumpet is again very active rhythmically in bars 13 and 14 before leaving space.

The comp uses the same voicings in bar 13 and 14 as in bars 9 and 10. Each chord is sustained for most of the measure behind the trumpet activity. Anticipating a space in the solo in bar 15, the comp uses a harmonized B♭ Dorian scale in an eighth note figure executed with a pair of triads (D♭, E♭, D♭) and finally moving the top note, A♭, down a half step to G, creating an E♭7 voicing. In bar 16, a similar rhythmic and melodic figure is executed using parallel "Ma7th" voicings for A-9 and B-9 followed by a C triad and a D13+4♭9 voicing from the Diminished scale. The ♯4 of the D13 voicing moves down to the 3rd on the last beat of the measure.

Rhythmically the figure in bar 16 just fits with the trumpet melody. If the solo line had been any different, the comp would have been inappropriately busy.

Measures 17–20

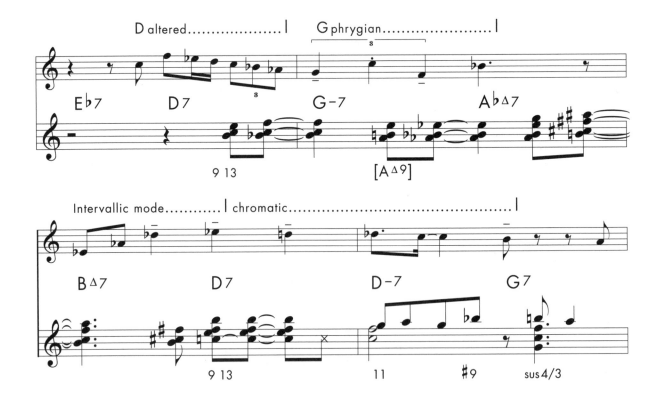

The soloist plays a descending Altered scale line over D7 in bar 17, leading to a fourths-based figure from the G Phrygian scale moving in contrast to the underlying harmony—the chords move up, the figure moves down. Consecutive fourths culminate in a ♭9 on the D7 in bar 19, descending chromatically into bar 20. The chromatic figure voice leads from the root, Δ7 and ♭7th of D-, resolving to the 3rd of G7.

Having played a busy figure at the end of the bridge, the comp rests at the top of the A section, only coming in to anticipate the G-7 in bar 18. Voicings made up of a 2nd and a 4th are used for G-7 (built on the the 3rd), AΔ7, A♭Δ7 (adding the 7th on top) and BΔ7. The D13 voicing in bar 19 is treated with contrapuntal right hand rhythm juxtaposing the top three notes and the bottom note.

Measures 21–24

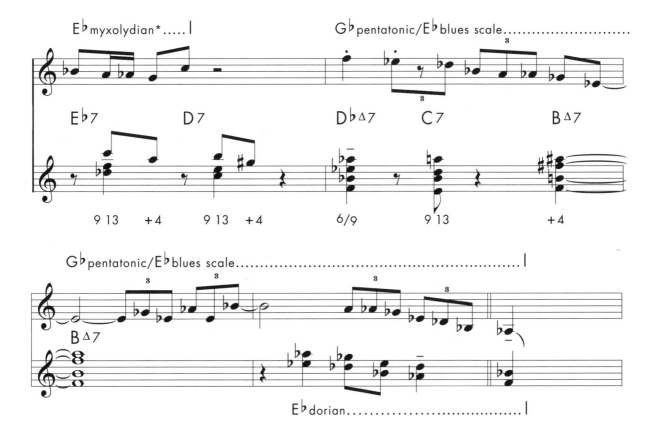

The trumpet solo resumes the chromatic line begun in bar 19, down to the 3rd of E♭7 then up a fourth. A G♭ Pentatonic/E♭ Blues scale umbrella is used over bars 22–24, beginning on beat 2. This is similar to the way in which the solo began, with a blues reference.

The comp continues with active rhythms, using moving notes to play the 13th down to the raised 4th of both the E♭7 and D7 chords. The four-note chords in bar 22 feature top voices ascending, in contrast with the descending roots. The rhythms used were predetermined as part of the arrangement. Bar 24 uses two-note voicings in response to the trumpet solo, and follows a G♭ Pentatonic scale until the first bar of the next chorus.

Modal Tune

Analysis starts on page 128.

This composition in based on one chord/scale only. When comping in this situation, voicings in fourths are ubiquitous, and the use of superimposed tonalities to create resolution patterns is common. The recording and transcription cover the last 32 bars of the solo.

Intro

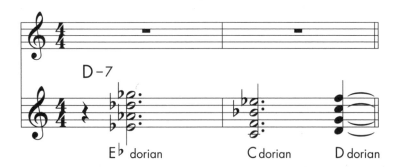

The soloist is leaving space until the beginning of the next 8-bar section. The guitar is playing chords that will create a resolution to the underlying D-. Parallel voicings in fourths with the top note outlining an interval found within the A Diminished scale (implying the dominant of the underlying key center). The rhythm (also used later in this piece) is a hemiola with dotted half notes, implying a tempo modulation. This rhythmic device creates tension without playing rhythms that conflict with the soloist.

Measures 1–8

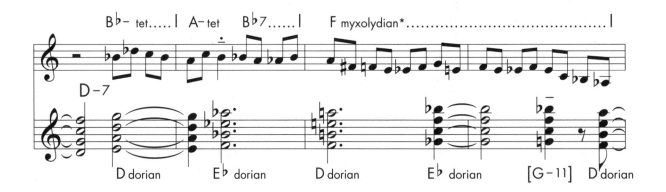

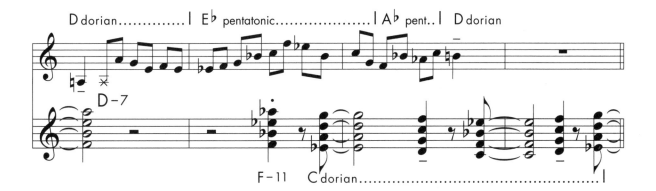

The first phrase of the solo uses a B♭- tetrachord resolving to A, the 5th of D-, which begins an A- tetrachord at the beginning of bar 2. A chromatic approach figure based on the root and 7th of B♭7 at the end of bar 2 again resolves to A, this time beginning an extended F Myxolydian figure with chromatic tones added. (This is the same scale as C Dorian, but the melody is built around F7.) The end of this line acts as a chromatic approach (above and below) to the 5th of D- on the downbeat of bar 5.

This voice leading provides a sense of logic and resolves the extended harmony in a musical way. In bars 5 and 6, an E♭ pentatonic structure ascending in sequence from the root to the 6th followed by a fourths motif through the first two beats of bar 7. The E♭ pentatonic resolves momentarily to A♭, which in turn resolves to the 6th of the underlying key center. The phrase rests in bar 8. The lines found in bars 1-16 are examples of an approach in which small structures such as tetrachords, pentatonic fragments and chromatic passing tones are used to create long, complex melodic lines (see *Jazz Guitar Structures*)

The guitar comp continues from the end of the previous phrase into bar 1 with a voicing in fourths (D, G, C, F) that constitutes the tonic of the key center, D Dorian. This voicing, along with the voicing built on the 3rd degree of the Dorian scale (F, B, E, A), are used exclusively in this eight bar phrase but are frequently transposed to other keys to approximate the sound of the altered dominant of the key. This device is used to create tension and interest within the comp and match the soloist's use of structures outside of the basic scale. Frequent key choices for transposition are E♭ Dorian, C Dorian, D♭ Dorian, A♭ Dorian, B♭ Dorian, etc. These scales all feature notes that are not found within the underlying D Dorian scale (to varying degrees).

Measures 1–8, continued...

In bars 1–8, the voicings are drawn primarily from the harmonized D Dorian scale and the harmonized E♭ Dorian scale. The first two voicings are from D Dorian; the voicing with A♭ in the melody is built on the second degree of E♭ Dorian. The voicing on the downbeat of bar 3 is built on the third degree of D Dorian; the next voicing is built on the third degree of E♭ Dorian. The G-11 chord is from the G Dorian scale. The top note of the this voicing (B♭) resolves to the A on the top of the subsequent voicing from D Dorian. After leaving space, the previous two-chord pattern is repeated down a whole step (F Dorian to C Dorian), with the remaining chords in bars 7 and 8 drawn from C Dorian.

Measures 9–16

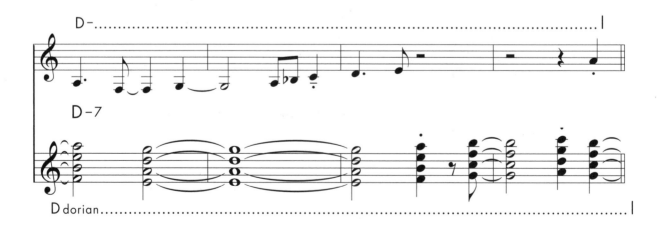

The trumpet solo features a tone row (using every chromatic pitch once each) in bars 9 and 10. This is another way to imply different harmonies over the underlying scale while maintaining organization. This is followed in bar 11 by another use of F Myxoldian with chromatic passing tones added to approach the 3rd on beat two of bar 11; the 7th on beat three; and the 7th again on beat one of bar 12.

The soloist ends the complex line with chromatic approaches to the 5th on the downbeat of bar 13. The subsequent melodic line is very much in the tonic key of the tune but uses B♭ instead of B natural found within the Dorian scale. The contrast of very chromatic lines with less complex statements and the use of space allows the listener to "digest" what has been heard.

The comp picks up with the voicing held over from bar 8, built on the 3rd of C Dorian. The feeling created by this superimposition is one of non-resolution at the end of the previous phrase, and this dovetails with the soloist's melodic statement in bars 9–12.

There is much use of space in the comp behind a very active, chromatic solo, puctuating only once in bar 10. The voicings moving chromatically at the end of bar 12 create a resolution pattern. In line with the soloist, voicings from the tonic scale are used in bars 13–16. A sustained chord built on the 2nd degree creates space in the middle of the phrase, followed by a motif, using voicings built on the 4th and 5th degrees of the scale, that will carry over into the next section and fills in the space at the end of the trumpet phrase.

The rhythms used at the end of the previous sections feature an attack on beat three followed by an attack on the "and" of four; in fact, all sections end with anticipation of the downbeat by a half step. In this instance however, the attack on beat three is followed by an attack *on* beat four which creates even greater propulsion rhythmically.

Measures 17–24

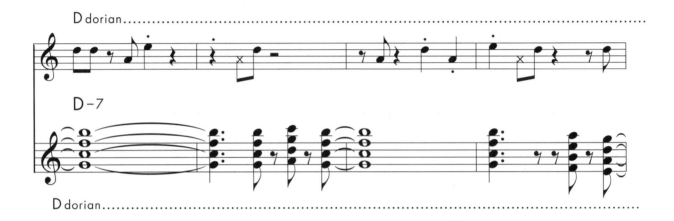

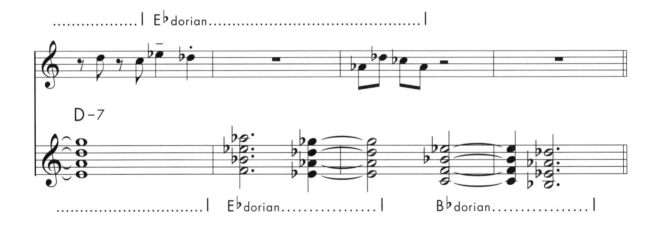

After the complexity of the previous 16 bars, the soloist plays a relatively simple and highly effective motivic section. Taking a rhythmic approach, a four-note melody built from within the tonic key is used in bars 17–20, and "answered" in bars 21–23 with material transposed up a half step to E♭ Dorian. Space is left in the last bar of the section to set up the final phrase of the solo.

The motivic/rhythmic approach allows for a greater degree of overt interaction between the soloist and the rhythm section, including the comper. Compare this with the first 16 bars, in which the comp uses sustain to create a harmonic backdrop and features active rhythms only at the end of a 4- or 8-bar section.

Behind this motivic section the comp uses chords built from the tonic scale (much like the solo), and responds to the trumpet changing scales in bar 21, also by using E♭ Dorian. The two pairs of parallel voicings used in bars 22–24 feature a melody outlining a G♭ pentatonic scale, and are drawn from E♭ Dorian and B♭ Dorian, respectively. This is another example of stating a tonic sound, then changing to a scale that can act as an implied Dominant in order to create tension and a resolution back to the tonic.

The rhythm continues the motif started in bar 15, this time using three consecutive off-beat attacks (the "and" of beats two, three and four). This rhythm fills in the space in the trumpet motif in bars 18 and 20, before returning to the hemiola rhythm that was used at the beginning of this 32 bars of trumpet solo, and which continues into the next 8-bar section.

Measures 25–32

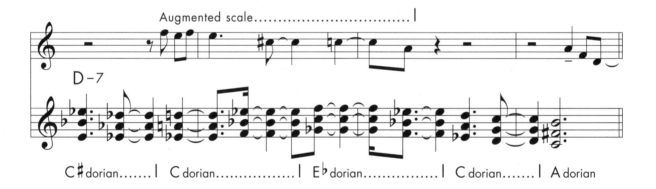

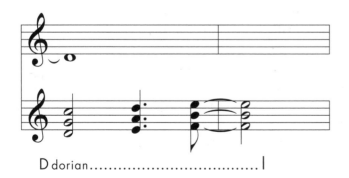

The soloist plays an ascending motif from the E pentatonic ♭2 scale, at first on beats one and three, then increasing the frequency of attack. After leaving space, the Augmented scale (alternating minor 3rds and half steps) is used to create a descending melody featuring a brief hemiola. The solo ends with a closing statement in the tonic scale.

The comp continues the hemiola begun in bar 22 with pairs of voicings from Dorian scales moving by minor thirds. The voicings over the first six beats are built on the third and fourth degrees of B♭ Dorian; the next two chords are built on the same degrees of C♯ Dorian.

At this point, the hemiola happens twice as fast, using dotted eighths instead of dotted quarters. The voicing pattern continues up another minor third to E Dorian and descends after the second voicing in the pair, through the voicing built on the 4th degree of B♭ Dorian in the middle of bar 29.

Keeping the lowest note the same, the scale set then shifts up a whole step to C Dorian/E♭ Dorian/C Dorian/A Dorian, while keeping the voicing pattern consistent. (The rhythm varies in bars 29–30 to reflect the comp "laying back" in the time, rather than actually metrically extending these attacks by a sixteenth note.) The long hemiola finally resolves on the downbeat of the next section.

The trumpet and guitar align perfectly on beat two of bar 27, with the comp doubling the speed of the hemiola at the same time as the trumpet melody becomes more active rhythmically. The comp maintains the tension while the trumpet rests, the trumpet then picks up the minor third motif of the comp in playing the Augmented scale. This is an instance of the soloist listening and responding to what is happening in the comp. By implying an extended altered Dominant chord and using rhythms that create motion without conflicting with the soloist, the comp achieves the effect of ratcheting up the level of tension and excitement through the culminating 8-bar phrase of the solo.

CD CONTENTS